ICON

Jack Smith

Books by Jack Smith

Co-authored with Eddie J. Girdner. *Killing Me Softly: Toxic Waste, Corporate Profit, and the Struggle for Environmental Justice*, Monthly Review Press, 2002.

Hog to Hog, Texas Review Press, 2008.

Write and Revise for Publication: A 6-Month Plan for Crafting an Exceptional Novel and Other Works of Fiction, Writer's Digest Books, 2013.

ICON

Jack Smith

SERVING HOUSE BOOKS

Icon

ISBN: 978-0-9913281-3-0

Cover design: Jack Smith and Walter Cummins

Serving House Books logo by Barry Lereng Wilmont

Published by Serving House Books
Copenhagen, Denmark and Florham Park, NJ
www.servinghousebooks.com

Member of The Independent Book Publishers Association

First Serving House Books Edition 2014

To Mary Jane Smith

Acknowledgments

I especially want to thank Penny Smith-Parris, Mark Wisniewski, and DeWitt Henry for their great encouragement on an early draft of this novel.

"I suggest that we build a big bronze and granite monument, a statue to honor some truly American heroes, unsung American heroes ... the rich."
—Bernard Goldberg

PART ONE

BLOOD SACRIFICE

1

It was Sheila Bozeman he had come to see at this beach hotel, Sheila his old college flame, Sheila who had somehow found out where he was, and then had informed him that she had broken up with her investor husband, was now divorced—and him, he had never married? Did she hear him correctly?

"That's right," said Peter, "I never did."

"God," she said. "Well, do we dare? Do we? After all these years?" She twirled around. "What do I look like to you—now?"

Slim as ever. Liquid blue eyes. Assertive chin.

But changed somehow. What exactly was the essence of this change? He searched his mind.

"You're—so tall. I hadn't remembered you so tall."

"I was always tall."

"That's nice. I'm excessively hungry—ravenous, and I guess it's that time. Isn't it?"

They headed to the restaurant.

A hostess steered them over to a table overlooking the beach. The bluish sky was pasted with white splotches of clouds with no apparent destination. In the distance you could see sailboats.

"Drinks?" said the waitress. She was a young thing. Her voice was sweet. Alluring, thought Peter.

"Vodka," said Shelia.

"Wine. Red."

Sheila brightened. "Nice view. What have you been doing with your life?" she suddenly asked. "For . . . what is it, fifteen years?"

"Professor," he said. "Of icons."

"Yes, yes, I *know* that. I saw you on the university website. My, my. Icons—you're still on *that* kick. What *is* it about those things?" She studied him closely. "Is that all you do?"

"Pretty much," he said. "What about you?"

"Bad marriage. But I told you that."

He nodded. She was staring at him. She had the habit of looking directly in your eyes, and not flinching.

"You did."

"And you never married. I just can't believe it."

"It's true."

"I guess I was the one, then, wasn't I? The only woman for Mr. Peter Boatz." She took his hand.

"We did hit it off pretty well back in those days, didn't we?" he said.

She withdrew her hand, gradually. "But who knows about those days? They were so . . . so strange. So odd. Weren't they?"

"Strange? Odd?"

"Yes, strange. Odd. We didn't know a single thing about the world, Peter. Neither me nor you. But it was fun. It was fun, those days of not knowing a single thing about the world. You find out though. You sure do find out."

The waitress came with the drinks.

Peter went for his wine. Such a young thing, that waitress— eyes like blue buttons. Fresh like a spring flower. He couldn't help but watch her as she walked off.

Sheila had taken his hand again.

"You're up to your old tricks," she said. "Aren't you?"

"What tricks?"

She shook her head, grinned to herself.

They drank their drinks.

Sheila talked about things she was currently doing, and got a little too detailed, for his taste anyway, on some local issues— including the tax base of their city, an industrial free zone problem for a corporation hoping to settle there, and huge bridge, road, and sewer projects—"Lots of infrastructure changes in our city," she said, brightly.

It seemed odd to him that after all these years, this particular topic of conversation would dominate their time together. He blurted out, "Look, Sheila—"

"Yes? What?"

"Those *were* good days, weren't they?"

She glared at him. He fell into those liquid blue eyes.

"You broke up with me. What was good about them?"

They were silent, drinking their drinks.

"But—"

"Oh, Peter, I've changed a lot in all those years. I doubt we'd have anything in common at all now. For instance, when I was talking about what's going on in our city, I saw your eyes glaze over. You weren't interested a bit in it. Were you?"

"Then why get together?"

"Curiosity."

The waitress arrived and took their orders. Sheila ordered a ten-ounce T-bone steak.

"Steak? Red meat?"

"Yes. I love it. I *devour* it."

"It's bad for you."

"So who cares?"

"Well."

"What are you—vegetarian or something?"

"Yes."

"Well, go ahead and be. But leave me to my red meat. Okay?"

"Sure."

"Besides, you used to eat a lot of meat, didn't you?"

"That was a long time ago."

"Well, bully for you. I thought jocks ate meat, and once a jock always a jock, right?" She grinned, then looked out the window.

He decided to eat, say it's been nice, and head up to his room.

"Still playing basketball?"

"No."

"What do you want out of life, Peter?"

"Pardon?"

"It's not such a hard question."

He sat forward. "Pretty personal. Isn't it?"

"We *were* personal."

"I don't know."

"Professor of icons. You were so given to those things, weren't you? Icon this, icon that. What's *representative*? What's abstract?

What's not? I got so tired of all that, to be honest. But, of course, that wasn't *all* you were thinking about," she whispered. "You were also thinking about something *else*. Weren't you?"

"*What?*"

"Icons—and *that*. Talk about getting stuck in a groove. I didn't think you'd *ever* get tired of *it*. Of *talking* about it. *Doing* it." She had turned to grinning and whispering.

"What the hell?" he said. "I was a kid. What else would I talk about?"

She looked away, a frozen grin on her lips.

"You talked about it too," he said.

She was still looking away, out the plate glass window onto the beach. Fleshy creatures pranced, splashed, and milled about in the water.

"Did you hear what I said?"

"What? Oh—sorry. I was drifting off there for a moment."

The waitress arrived with the food. "Refills?"

"Yes," said Peter.

"Say, this looks good, doesn't it?"

"You used to talk about it too," he said.

"What?"

"*It*," he whispered. "You used to talk about *it*. We both did, not just me."

"Oh, well," she said, and began cutting her steak into cube-size pieces. "Who could blame me—with such a jock?" She ate, her attention on her steak, and then looked up at him, swallowing. "I suppose you think you're going to bed me down again," she whispered.

He sat back. "*What!*"

"To make up for all you missed . . ."

"Are you serious?"

"Not going to happen. I'm here to visit, and that's it. Okay?" She delivered a cube of steak to her mouth and licked her lips. "I *did* want to see you. I was surprised you live only one hundred miles from here. Fancy that."

"But a mistake," said Peter. "Wasn't it?"

14

"You *were* thinking about it, though, weren't you? That's why you showed up. Admit it."

He shook his head. "I'm not dignifying that."

"I'm lonely, Peter, but I'm not desperate. I've got a life, you know, and I do quite well—on my own."

Fifteen minutes, he thought. Half hour, tops.

She resumed eating. "You *are* anxious. I can tell. You want to bring it all back, don't you?"

"You called *me*. As you might recall."

"Why ever did I do that?"

"I don't know—why?"

"You *want* to," she said. "But I'm not up for it." She continued to look at him.

"Okay," he said. "I'd like to. My room or yours?"

"Neither."

He ate while she chattered on—about her work for city government, about *them*, about how she didn't really mean half of what she said, she was just all confused right now, and she was happy to see him and wanted to meet him in the morning for breakfast.

"Eight," she said. "Will you be up by then?"

"Of course."

She patted his hand. "I did love you," she said. "In spite of everything."

He got a buzz. But maybe it was the wine.

The next morning as he entered the restaurant, he saw her seated with two other people, and she motioned him over, excitedly.

"Peter, meet my two dear friends, Bob and Lee!"

Bob, a large man with massive arms and a pencil-line mustache, rose from his chair. He extended a hand, and they shook.

He had the distinct air of an insurance salesman. How was that? Peter couldn't say why. Perhaps it was that strong odor of minty aftershave?

"Pleasure, Peter. This is Lee, my wife."

"Hi, Peter." Lee remained seated. She was as small as Bob was large. He'd squash her, thought Peter.

"They are my closest, dearest friends."

"Sit down, Peter," said Bob.

The waitress arrived. "What are we having?"

"You two order, and then Peter and I will order," said Sheila.

"Oh, nothing much," said Bob. "Let's see. I'll take a number six, I guess."

"How do you want your eggs?"

"Scrambled. Double it."

"Yes, sir. Done. Ma'am?"

Lee looked preoccupied. "I don't know. Oh, Bob, just order for me. I don't have the slightest. I guess I'm not exactly hungry. I don't know."

"Give her the number five," said Bob. "She'll like that."

"Okay, great," said the waitress. And she turned to Peter. "Sir?"

"Coffee," said Peter. "Just coffee."

"Aren't you a breakfast eater?" asked Bob. He laid a hand on Peter's shoulder. He rested it there.

"Coffee's fine."

"He's upset," said Sheila. "I can tell that look. Don't you think? He looks *peeved*, doesn't he?"

"Pardon?" said Peter.

"Peeved," said Sheila. She winked at him.

Bob laughed. "My god, Peter, *women*. How they do read us. Right?"

"I wouldn't know about that."

"What do you want, ma'am?" said the waitress.

"Me? I'll take a number fifteen. I'll bet he would too if he wasn't so *peeved*."

"Sir?" said the waitress, smiling.

"Coffee is fine."

"Party poop," said Sheila.

"Peter, don't pay her any mind," said Bob. "She's just funning with you."

"Bob's right," said Lee. "We know our Sheila." She took hold of

Sheila's arm and gave her a peck on the cheek.

Sheila was staring at him, about to laugh. There was a come-hither look on her face—he recognized it from the old days.

Bob launched out into some story. Peter had trouble following it. When Bob asked him something, he noticed everyone looking at him. "What?"

"Don't you think so?"

"Think what?"

"He's off in his own little world," said Sheila, "as always." She burst forth with a big smile. There was something behind it. Suddenly the mystery was cleared up. He saw the blood red blossom of her cheek—he'd missed it before. What did this represent? A blossom like that? He didn't know, but he wanted her in ways he couldn't have predicted.

"What I was *saying*," said Bob, "was that your average guy out there has a fear of heights. Your average guy has a fear of depths. Your average guy has a fear of snakes, bears, tigers, alligators, sharks. Semi-trucks, private planes. Out of control government. But do you know that your average guy—I'm drawing on a study here, Peter, from some psychology journal or something, don't ask me which one, I forget that sort of thing—your average guy has a fear, a mindless sort of numbing fear, of *sameness*. It's not just boredom. It's raw, primal *fear*."

"But is that really *fear*, honey?" asked Lee.

"It is," said Bob. "According to this study."

"Studies like that are rather suspect," said Sheila. "Aren't they?"

"Perhaps so," said Bob. "But one of the authors was a Nobel laureate. It's the kind of fear that comes with retirement, being shelved, you see. Having nothing, absolutely nothing, to do. Some guys would rather be tortured than have nothing, absolutely nothing, to do. Odd, isn't it?"

"I still think," said Lee, "that that sounds more like boredom than fear."

"I'm with Lee," said Sheila.

"Peter?" said Bob.

"I'm not sure," said Peter. "It does sound suspect." He made a mental note to record this conundrum in his pocket-size journal.

"Isn't the beach beautiful this morning?" said Sheila. "God, but look at that fat woman! Why would you go out and expose such flabby flesh to the entire gazing world?"

"We're off the topic," said Bob.

"We're tired of the topic," said Sheila.

"So what do you do, Peter?" said Bob.

"He's a professor," said Sheila. "Of icons."

"A professor of *what*?"

"Icons."

"Ah!" Bob raised a finger to his nose. "I see now. And I am *reminded*. Did you hear about this guy who's building a monument to the rich—or rather a monument to *spite* the rich?" He looked around. "Did you? Yes, this is what he is doing. A huge, huge—"

Lee touched his arm. "Let's don't talk about that, honey. I really don't think these two—"

"I'm quite interested," said Peter.

"You hate the rich?" said Sheila.

Bob laughed. "This man—they call him Mr. Finger—says, when completed, the spiteful monument will be a gigantic finger a half mile high." He raised his hand way above the table. "Just imagine. Giving the rich the finger a half mile high!"

"It's so dreadful, really," said Lee.

"My god," said Sheila. "He's certainly going for it in a big way. What would such a thing cost?"

"Millions. But then he's had several million donations of one to a thousand bucks a pop. The Internet is a fantastic organizer, as we all know."

"That many people hate the rich?"

"People have always hated the rich," said Bob. "Even the rich hate the rich. Of course as far as that goes, the poor hate the poor." He seemed to disappear into his double order of scrambled eggs. But suddenly he stood up. "You know, I could use a swim myself." Bob was exceedingly tall, even taller than he. He worked his pencil-line mustache with an idle finger. "Yes, I think I'll take a short swim. Lee?"

"Not me. I'll stay put with Sheila."

"I'll stay put with Lee."

"Peter?"

"Maybe."

He drank down his coffee.

"No *fierce* swimming. Just see what the water's like."

"I know why he's going out there," said Lee.

"And why is that?" said Sheila.

"To get a better view. Take a look."

They all looked out, and two teenage girls were performing an exercise, or dance steps, within fifteen feet of the restaurant window.

"Let's go," said Bob.

"Better hurry," said Lee.

"Is he always this way?" said Sheila.

"Oh, worse. Give me a kiss," Lee said and held her cheeks up for Bob to plant one on her. He kissed her two quick ones. "Bye, now," he said.

Sheila laughed.

Peter followed Bob outside.

"That woman loves you, you know," said Bob. "And she's free."

"I heard," said Peter.

"She's a strange woman. That wretch she was married to— had his nose in his work. I'd say she's ripe for something else." He stopped and studied Peter. "She told us about you two. I'd say she's ripe. Ripe for the plucking."

2

He had met Sheila Bozeman, his old high school flame, on his way to the Student Union after pulling an all-nighter, writing an Icons paper: "The Icons of the Middle Ages: The Castle, the Virgin, and the Torture Chamber." *Dig deep*, said his professor. *Fullness, range—that's what I want.*

Fullness, range.

He had burned up his mind on it for weeks, and then the night before the paper was due, changed his thesis. Those icons, so slippery. Just when you thought you had them nailed—

All they suggested, all they didn't.

Pin it down, said the professor. *Pin it down, but allow room.*

He had pinned it down—just enough. And he'd allowed room.

Ah, and that was some relief.

As he was heading for the Student Union, there she was. He recognized the movements of her frame, the swing of her head, the way she got the hair off her forehead, her thick calves visible as she took a step upon the curb and started toward him.

He shouted to get her attention.

She stopped, stared.

"Me," he said. "Peter."

"Peter?"

"Me," he said.

"I didn't know you went here."

"Well, I do."

"You weren't going, though."

"You weren't either."

"No—I changed my mind at the last minute."

"So did I."

"Odd."

"Yes—odd, isn't it?"

"Why do you . . . look so silly?" she said.

"Silly?"

"That shirt."

It was hanging down under his coat, bunched up. An element of contemporary disorder? Or was it evidence of class behavior? Could it be both?

"I was up all night."

"Figures." She grew morose. "I've got class. Nice seeing you." She moved on.

"No, wait. Don't go."

"Don't *go*?"

"Skip class—please. Come with me."

"Are you crazy?"

"Come eat with me, and then we can fool around, okay?"

Bad choice of words.

"Fool around? Do it? Is that what you mean?"

"No. Of course not. You still sore about that?"

"Sore about what?"

"Nothing. Look, couldn't we go get something to eat or drink?"

"I'm so cold," she said. "I don't want to stand here talking."

"Let's get inside, then."

"No—go away. Please."

"Why? Come on," he pleaded.

They headed to the Union.

"I'm dying of hunger," she said.

She *looked* starved, acted starved, her face, her movements, but her body was the same, sumptuous. He'd begged for it in senior year. Finally, she'd relented. But it hadn't gone so well.

They ate and then they were back on the sidewalk.

"Why don't we go to *my* place?" He took hold of her.

She pulled loose. "Well, I can see that I guessed right. Now why would we do that, Peter?"

"Why shouldn't we?"

An ironic, mocking look crossed her lips. "You're just dying for it, aren't you? And you didn't even bother to find me—and I've been here for two whole stupid years!"

"I didn't know you were here."

"You might have checked. That'd be up to you, wouldn't it, being the man?"

"Come back with me. I'll make it up to you," he said, taking hold of her hand.

"Make it up to me?"

"Yes."

"Where is it? This big, special place?"

"Six blocks off."

"Where?"

"A house. Second floor."

"Somebody's house."

"But the old lady's not home—half the time."

"A room, I take it."

"Yes."

"Oh, my god."

"She works during the day. It's okay. I guarantee."

"Up in your room. That's where you want me."

"It's nice there."

"You are such a stupid jock."

"No, no," he said. "I'm not doing well in that at all."

"Doesn't change anything," she said. "Once a jock, always a jock."

"I'm tall, but I'm not much good at it," he said. "But—"

"What?"

He told her all about his icons. He was changing. He was turning intellectual. "I'm much more mental now," he said.

"I think I like the jock more," she said.

They came to the house. It was quiet inside, no one on the stairs. The guy on the third floor, a graduate student who drank a lot and womanized—no sign of him. They ascended the stairs. Peter stuck his key in, turned it quickly, and pushed open the door. She grimaced, but went in. He shut the door and locked it.

She was his.

She sat on the narrow, unmade bed. Dust bunnies floated against the baseboard. He went to the apartment-size refrigerator and grabbed two beers. "Want one?"

"What? At this time of the morning?"

"How about Coke?"

"Okay."

He brought out two.

She grabbed one.

The mood had dampened somehow.

She drank her Coke and stared at him. "How's basketball?"

"That? Okay. Well . . . not okay really."

"Can't dribble?"

"Or shoot. Free throws, especially. Free throws are tough."

"You get nervous."

"Yeah, but—"

"What?"

"There's more."

"Tell me."

It was hard to explain. "Ideas. I start thinking all kinds of things out there, especially when it's free throw time. I try not to, but they just come at me. You know?"

"No, I don't. What things?"

"All kinds. I can't even begin—"

"Do begin."

"Okay. Big ideas—philosophical ideas, history, psychology, sociology, high-level math—prodding me, demanding answers. Like understanding Kantian deontology, or B.F. Skinner, or differential equations . . . it's weird. Real weird. But it's true."

"I'll just bet."

"No—it's true. It's like my mind goes in overdrive. Working that stuff I'm studying in my courses. You know what it was last game?"

"*Practice* game, you mean?"

"Yeah."

"Well, what was it?"

"It was two geometric shapes. I had to know—to figure out the answer."

"What answer?"

"The volume of a specific trapezoid minus a particular parallelogram."

"You were thinking about that at the free throw line."

"Yep."

"Maybe it's something pathological," said Sheila.

"You mean I'm sick?"

"Maybe. Maybe you ought to see a doctor about it."

"I don't know. But I'll say one thing: You can't play ball like that. That's for sure. But I can't quit. It's the scholarship money."

"You thinking about something right now?" she asked.

"Huh?"

"Are you thinking about *something else*?"

"What do you mean?"

"*Other* than me?"

"No. Oh, no."

"You better not be. How're classes?"

"Good. I'm studying really hard."

"I'm making C's and B's. I suppose you're making A's."

"I hope so. My paper on the major icons of the Middle Ages—I ought to ace that."

"Which icons?"

"The castle, the Virgin, and the torture chamber."

She shook her head. "Torture chamber? I suppose that turned you on, huh? You chose that?"

"The cross and the rack."

"How dismal."

"My field of expertise," he said. "Or *will* be—some day. You just watch. I'm on fire. I'm at my flash point! All kinds of icons I'm pursuing: Ancient, Modern, Contemporary!"

"You rehearsed that, didn't you?" said Sheila, looking dead on at him. "What in heaven's name do you do with icons? Teach, I guess. How many are there? Thousands? Millions?"

"There are certain key ones," said Peter. "I could list several."

"Don't bother. I just want to drink my Coke. Please."

She was still sore. But he would change that. Look how much she had already warmed up.

He could tell when a girl was warming up. He'd had a few up here in the room, though nothing much had happened. That guy upstairs, though. He heard girl voices up there half the time, and the deaf old landlady never caught him—not once. That was certainly propitious.

"Come here." She beckoned at him with her finger.

He moved quickly toward her.

"You want me," she said. "That's *it*, isn't it?" She spoke softly, under her breath.

"Yes." He saw into those liquid blue eyes.

He stood next to her on the bed, and he touched her shoulder, and then he moved closer and began kissing her neck. He wanted to gobble her up. It was like she was a rare piece of meat.

"God!" she yelled, shoving him off. "What are you, some kind of vampire!"

Rebuffed, he sat still.

She sipped her Coke.

"I just don't get it!" she cried. And then she dropped the Coke in a wastebasket and put on her coat, buttoned up, opened the door and slammed it on her way out.

He heard her on the landing and on the stairs half way down. He heard the front door jerk open and slam.

Trouble again with Sheila, his old flame in high school, and now he had to go see the coach—for more bad news. If you had to see the coach, it was bad news or good. With him, it was always bad.

The coach's door was partially open. Peter knocked on the metal door frame. He'd learned to knuckle it hard to make sufficient noise.

"Yeah! What is it?"

He waited while the coach bent down over some sort of paperwork. The coach didn't like his ball players to head straight for the Player Chair. Not until he'd pointed at it. Right now the coach was rubbing his red nose.

Then the coach looked up and pointed.

Peter took the Chair. The coach scowled at him. "What the hell's up with you? Why're you playing so fucking bad?"

The coach used the f-word a lot.

"I don't know."

"It's like you can't hit anything with that ball. Pete, I hate to say it—"

"Peter."

The coach looked like he'd been smacked. He sat forward abruptly. "Okay, *Peter*. Hell, maybe that's why you can't hit a goddamn thing with that ball. What kind of name is *Peter*?"

"It's my name."

"Okay . . . okay, we got that straight, son. But what's the deal here? What's going on? You're looking at a downward shift—fourth string's next. You want that?"

"No."

"But you don't care."

"Yeah, sure I do, but—"

"Go ahead. Spit it out. Jeez, Pete—Peter—just tell me. I'm your goddamn friend. I'm your coach. We're in this fucking thing together. Comprende?"

He beckoned Peter to scoot forward.

"Look at you. Look how tall you are—six two. Six fucking two! A young man six two like you, hell he ought to be able to shoot that ball wherever he wants. Right? *Wherever* he wants. And run down that court like he owns it."

"I'm not *that* tall for basketball. There's others that—"

"You're *tall* if I say you're tall. Hear?"

"Yeah."

"Who's the coach?"

"You, sir."

"You got your head up your ass, son. That's the problem. I look out there, and you're not present and accounted for. What's coming down—you on drugs, or something?"

"No, sir."

"What, then?"

"I don't know. I can't really—"

"You don't care."

"No, I do. I care." And he thought maybe he did care. Because part of him did want to be a ball player. To swish that thing right through the net. To stand halfway across the court—well, a third anyway—and shoot that thing so that it swished. *Swished.* Not hit the backboard, not hit the metal ring of the net—but *swished.* Man, that was about as good as it got, and on top of it, you'd get the girls. The girls went crazy over a guy who swished. A backboard guy didn't count as much. You could tell.

"Okay, okay. You care. Then you know what's expected, don't you?"

The coach gave him that expectant look. His red nose jutted out at him.

"Two hundred percent."

"There you go. One hundred percent first day, two hundred once you make the fucking team."

"I know."

"But you don't care."

"Yes, I do," said Peter. "I do care. I'll do better." Scholarship money. He had to.

"Fourth's not good, son. Not good at all."

The coach rose. Meeting concluded.

With a bit of coaxing, he got her back. With a little more coaxing, he got her to remove her clothes.

"I can't believe it," she said. "I can't *believe* I'm doing this."

Soon she made a habit of coming to his room every single afternoon. First, they would have something from his small refrigerator—ham sandwich, chips, Coke. And then they would get in his bed, and they would do it for an hour, sometimes even longer. "You just love my *flesh*, don't you?" she'd say. And then they would study together, both of them on the bed, dressed again, her putting on her large pink glasses he liked because they accented her rosy complexion, and then they would go out and take a walk, and then come back to the room again and have sex (twice in a day if he got his way), and then they would go out in the evening and have a nice meal at the Pub. Noisy, crowded with college kids, draught beer flowing freely, laughter infectious and seismic. And the young men noticed her. They thought she was a real looker, he could see it.

He liked to sit in a booth with her—just the two of them. Talk. Talk about many things. The ideas circulating in his brain. Icons, mainly. "It's such a vast, all-encompassing field," he told her. He wanted her to appreciate it. How it took in everything, as his professor was constantly crowing. "Think," he said, "just think, how something material comes to *mean* something—actually *mean* something. Isn't that fascinating, utterly fascinating? It's no longer just a thing anymore. A mere *thing*. Do you see? Do you?"

She let him go on and on, though she didn't seem to be paying all that much attention. One evening she put her finger up.

What was he going to do with all this when he finished college?

"Off to grad school."

"I know, I know. But after that—teach? Must you? Must you really?"

"Yes. Of course."

"You'll be poor. Always poor."

"I don't care," he said.

"You will. Even if you don't care now."

"I want things to mean something," he said. "I want a meaningful sort of existence."

"Where'd you get that?"

"Well."

"From that professor of yours?"

He looked away from her. What was wrong with quoting his professor?

"You and your icons," she said, jabbing the table with her finger. A slim, feminine finger, and it turned him on. "It all seems pretty stupid to me. All these professors professing stuff no one can possibly use. I'd like to know the point of it all."

He had a flash. "You're still on the pill," he said. "*Aren't* you?"

It was like he'd smacked her. She sat forward. "Yes, I'm *on* the pill. That hasn't changed in the last week. God. You ask such questions!"

"Okay, okay."

"If you ask me that again," she said.

"I won't."

"I'll bet you do. I'll just bet. Probably before the night's over."

"No. Sorry."

"And so what if I wasn't?"

"What?"

"What if I *wasn't*?"

"If you weren't?"

"That's what I said. If I wasn't."

"Oh, god," he said.

"What if I *did* have a baby? Would that be so bad?"

"What? Yes? Yes! It would be!"

"Why?"

"I don't have a job!"

"We could have a little one," she said. "Even so."

"A little one?" He felt suddenly helpless. Shaky.

"Yes. And what's wrong with a little one?"

"Now? Right now?"

"What's the *point* of it?" she said. "You tell me the *point* of it if it's not that? You're the big deep thinker!"

"What?"

"Biology," she said. "Isn't that the point of it all?"

"I guess."

"You guess?"

"But now?"

"Oh, fuck you!" she shouted. She hurried off. She left half a beer standing. He sat there in his booth in the Pub, finished her beer and ordered another pitcher, and got stumbling drunk. He wandered back to his room alone, shivering. He felt the heavy air of desertion in the cold room.

He kicked at dust bunnies.

A light rain drizzled down the window. A life gone, a life passed. He'd had it all, but now he'd blown it.

And then it suddenly occurred to him—god, it was *that*. Of course it was. Sure, it was. Damn right, it was.

The next morning he headed out. He shoved his gloveless hands in the deep pockets of his pea coat.

He met her at her door. She looked broken. She'd been crying. Two roommates were curled on their beds reading.

"I will meet you out *there,*" she said.

She meant the Lounge. He went through the double doors and took a place on a couch.

He thumbed a magazine.

It was ten minutes.

She sat down beside him.

"Are you pregnant?" he burst out. "You are, aren't you?"

She didn't answer—not at first. Her chin trembled. "What?" she said.

"*Pregnant!*"

She shoved him. She stood up. "Why in the hell?"

"Huh?"

"Why in the *hell*?"

"What?"

"Why in the damn hell would you ask me that? Why the fuck!"

"I just thought, what with you—"

"Oh, I get it. I get it! That again! You think I haven't been taking the pill. You think you have to check on me and check on me and check again on me to make sure I'm still taking the fucking pill! Well, I *am* taking the fucking pill! But a lot of good it will do you because I won't be doing it with *you* anymore!"

A couple of girls had just burst through the double doors. They put their hands over their mouths. They giggled.

She was glaring down at him.

"Not so *loud,*" he whispered.

"I don't have anything to hide," she shouted.

"But what . . . what—"

"So you're free to go screw and screw and screw as much as you want—just not me! I'm not some sort of blood sacrifice!"

It was a good two weeks before he got her to come around.

That winter was snow and slush and ice, and winter winds, which turned to spring and balmy air. He spoke to her again of his dreams—she seemed to have sweetened with the spring weather. "I will understand the nature of icons," he said. "Like my professor says, think of icons as your major pillars, holding the whole structure up. If you understand your icons, you know what it all means. Maybe you don't know all the particulars, but that's not important. Not really. You know the big or general stuff." She was listening, though she seemed somewhat distracted the more he went on, which made him want to go on further—to be sure she understood. He knew he was being melodramatic, but your girlfriend—she ought to understand a thing like that. And so he really laid it on: "Everything about me," he said, "it's all centered around this icon business. See, I want to know the abstract. The interplay of abstraction with the concrete, the universal in the particular, the symbol—the culturally iconic!"

It was right out of his professor's lectures.

"Really?" she said. She toyed with her beer tab.

"It charges me up," he said.

"Yeah? As much as me?"

He saw the trap. "Of course it's not *that* good, of course not."

He waited a day, and then went on. He told her of the Millennial Icon Conference he hoped to attend in London. You had to work out intricate relations between a half dozen contemporary icons. You had to have the icons graphically represented, discuss each at length, the complexities, the intricate subtleties, the contextual features—

"Oh? And what do you think your coach will say about all that?"

"Coach? Screw the coach!" he yelled. "I'm done with the coach!"

"How about your *scholarship* money? You done with that?"

"No, but I go through the motions, all mechanical, acting like I give a damn—it's all a ruse. Ha!"

"When you don't. You don't give a damn at all."

"No."

"Is that a fact? You don't care about much of anything, do you, other than that stupid icon stuff!"

"No—I care. I care."

"I want babies!" she cried out. "Lots of babies!"

"Huh?"

"You heard me." Her voice broke.

"What?"

"That's *me,*" she said. "You said it for *yourself.* That's me. Is that so bad?" She began to cry—silently.

"I know," he said. He patted her.

"But you don't care, do you? You don't care about me—not really."

"Yes, I do," he said. "Sure I do."

She seemed to warm up at that. "See," she said, "I just want something to show for it all. Don't you think that makes sense? That I would want that?"

"Sure. It makes perfect sense."

"No, it doesn't—not to you. *Nothing* is real to you. Just a bunch of books and *doing* it. Like some kind of animal!"

"No, no. I like babies," he said. "Babies are good—they're fun."

She gave him a look. "Yeah? How would you know? You ever even *held* a baby?"

No. He had to admit it—not once.

"I suppose you like the *idea* of a baby," she said. "Is that it?"

"What else could I like, if I don't know any *real* babies?"

"Would you like to have a baby with me? A *real* baby?"

He nodded. He sure wouldn't ask the *now* question.

"Well," she said. "And when would you like to have this baby?"

"When?"

"Quit that!"

"I'm sorry. Well, I guess when we're ready for it. Get finished with school, you know. Get married."

She started to come undone. She went into some sort of fetal position on his bed.

"I want some kind of life!" she screamed. "Now! I want some kind of life! Is that too much to ask?"

He wrote it off to trouble with grades, hormones, and worries about the future. And of course she was the emotional type to begin with.

He tried to help. "It's okay," he said. "It's okay."

"I don't want to wait forever!"

He tried to console her.

"You're using me," she said.

"No," he said. "It's mutual, isn't it? I thought it was mutual."

Do you know that my Biology professor made a move on me?"

"Huh? What move? What?"

"He sure did."

"When? Where?"

"Oh, don't get so excited. It was last fall. I was in his office. He was acting kind of weird. I was sitting with my legs crossed. I had on a kind of short skirt, and I guess I showed too much leg. And he placed his hand on my knee. Right *there*." She took his hand and put it there. "I pushed his hand away, and I took off. I could hear him hurrying out of his office, the door making a racket, and pretty soon, I felt this hand grabbing my arm."

She stared at him.

"And?" said Peter.

"Petrified. The poor bastard looked absolutely petrified. I mean it. Said, 'I didn't ... I didn't mean ... to do that. A mistake. It was a terrible mistake.' Stumbled all over the place, couldn't get it out hardly. I said, 'Yeah? That was hardly a mistake!' He said, 'Please, please, don't report ... don't report this to anybody, please. I've got a wife, three kids—it would ruin me. Absolutely ruin me.' Blah, blah, blah—you know the drill. I thought he was going to cry. You know what? I laughed. 'You never can tell *what* might happen with a thing like this,' I said, and I left him to imagine the worst on his own. You know what?"

"What?"

"I had a D going into the final?"

"Yeah?"

"Mostly because of that stupid fucking lab—and I got an A out of that course. What do you think about that?"

"D."

"Barely that."

33

"My god."

She drank her beer. "D to A. Now how about that?"

"Maybe you made an A on the final."

"You serious? I didn't know crap about that class. Biology? I didn't know anything. And I got an A. I got a fucking A."

"Hmmm," he said.

"Not bad for one moment of being groped, is it?"

"You didn't see him again?"

"You mean did I threaten him?"

"Yes."

"No. I didn't say a word. But he sure tried to avoid me in class. Never called on me—not once. Wouldn't even look at me."

"Must have been pretty bad."

"For whom?"

He paused.

"For *you*," he said.

"No, that's not what you meant. You meant for *him*. Because being a man, you'd just naturally take his side, wouldn't you? Especially since he's a *professor*—your type."

"Oh, no . . . it was *his* fault. He sexually assaulted—"

"You're damn right he did! He'd of screwed me right there on his desk if thought he could get away with it!"

"Bad," he said. "Bad."

"Score settled," she said.

"Well," he said.

"You," she said. "Another professor. That's what you'll do, isn't it? Go after some sweet little thing like me? Feel her up. Screw her if you get a chance."

The angry, malicious Sheila. Clawing, biting.

"I wouldn't do that," he said softly.

"Your mind's on everything but me!" she said. "And I hate it!"

He calmed her down. She said she loved him, loved him, loved him. "That's why I act the way I do," she cried. "Don't you *see*? And don't you see this: that coital union must necessarily produce offspring? I am a baby-maker, by nature, Peter!"

"Where'd you get that?" he asked.

34

"Why is that important?"

"Where, though?"

"Something I read."

Baby-Maker, he thought. He couldn't help but work on that one—couldn't get it out of his head. Too bad that it worked on him when he was up for a free throw. He didn't even hit the backboard. The coach booted him down to fourth string.

He had to get away from Sheila Bozeman. He did when he graduated.

3

His second was a grad student like him. They got into it fast, and once again he began to worry about the biological realities. But there was no cause for alarm because this woman was a fierce pursuer of her own freedom, and she swore she had no time for children, though she had plenty of time for sex.

"Plenty," she said. "I really can't get enough of it, if you want to know."

"Oh," he said, and grew anxious.

"I'm serious. I'm dead serious."

This somehow alarmed him.

She moved in, within a week. He was certainly pleased to get all he wanted, though it began to occur to him that you could actually get too much. She had come to want it three to four times a day.

"Surfeit," he told her. "Like food, you can get too much sex. Right?"

"I don't think so," she said.

"Where is the limit, exactly?" he asked. "It probably varies with each man or woman."

"There's no strict mathematical formula," she said. "If there was, it would be variable surely. You must factor in mood, what you've had to eat, your recent thoughts, perceptual experiences of various kinds—the list goes on."

"Sex is important," he said. "But it isn't everything."

"Of course it is. Like breathing," she told him. "Essential *energy*." She would do it twenty-four hours a day if she didn't get sore. But three or four times a day—nice, fine, great. Once in the morning. Once in the afternoon. Once in the evening. Once late at night. "Is that too much to ask? God, I'm young, alive! I want to live. You see that, don't you?"

"Well, I'm young too," he said, "but hell . . . maybe I'm not quite up to it. But I'll try. I'll try."

"You better," she said.

He did, but there were embarrassing lacks of potency. He was in the middle of writing a thirty-five page paper on Francis Bacon as an Iconic Early Modern, and she stood behind him, kissing his ear.

He jerked away. How could he concentrate? Francis Bacon? Sexual liaison? What the hell?

"What's wrong?" she demanded.

"Nothing. Bacon."

"Bacon? Understood. An hour?"

"Sure. Of course. An hour."

"An hour is fine," she said. "But please—please don't postpone."

A sex schedule, he thought. Roughly every six hours, like clockwork.

He began to think of her as the Nymph.

The essence of a person's life, he thought, is the mind. To fuel the mind, what do we need? Food, drink, rest. Sex, sure. But *food*— who could dispute it? One centers so much around it. And it struck him that at a recent grad party, she had inserted one cracker in her mouth, one morsel of cheese, and had taken a couple sips of wine. No more. He'd watched closely.

She ate so little.

Something wrong there, he thought. Something really wrong there.

Bacon paper due. Ten pages still to write. He had it sketched out in his mind. Merely a matter of racking it out. Ten-thirty, and he jotted down a tentative time-line:

Bacon till 11:30
Sex till 1:00
Bacon till 3:00
Polish Bacon till 7:00
Sex till 8:00
Dress by 8:30
Class at 9:00

You must be done with sex by 1:00, he instructed himself.

You must be done with sex by 8:00. But what if she wanted to experiment?

He asked about babies—the natural result of sex, the issue of coital reality.

"I hate babies. I utterly loathe them."

"You hate babies?"

"Yes, I hate babies. I hate their smell, their stink, their whining, crying, bawling, red-faced hysterics. If it was up to me, there wouldn't be one more baby in the world—*ever*. Sex without babies. The purpose of sex, according to the conventional wisdom of the old, the conservative, and even the liberal freako natural birth types—you know them—is that sex is all about procreation. Correction: enjoyment too, bonding one with the other, but *secondarily* enjoyment. *I* say sex is about *pleasure*. Pleasure only. If it has instrumental value, it's that and only that."

Sometimes, she could enter into such tirades. He knew she'd want a response. When he didn't respond, she called him Mr. Average Male, Mr. Silent.

"It's about pleasure," he said. "Of course it is. But what if there were *no* babies, not a one—to consider your idea here—not *one* more. Ever. Well, then, there would be no more sex."

She gave him an impatient shake of the head. "Irrelevant. Do we procreate so that others, not ourselves, will have pleasure? And what if I don't want babies? Am I somehow *obligated* to have them? To reproduce myself? Is this some sort of cosmic dictum? Do I want a little tyke—don't you just hate that word?—running around duplicating my *own* existence on this earth? Know what? There's something pernicious about that. It's sick, sick—sickness unto death."

"Wait a minute," he said, "that's Kierkegaard."

"And?" she said.

Sick? How could it be sick? He pushed the point.

"What choice do they have? Do they say: 'I'd like to enter that contagion called human existence? Be berated, fouled, diseased, hurt, punched, starved, bombed, shelled, tortured, mutilated, harassed, tested, papered to death, jobbed, paid, indebted, and end up in a box for all eternity'? Define that as you will. Do they?"

"God," he said. "God." In her sea of philosophical sharks, he saw a delightful boatload of icons. He tried to commit to memory half of what she'd said. He was quite tempted to take out his small notepad, but he usually waited until the conversation was over.

"You do see what I mean?"

"Yes, but how about other species?"

"Fish, fowl, the things that crawl upon the earth, the things that devour and are devoured?"

"Yes."

"Well, what do you think? What do you fucking think? I don't think any of them ever asked permission, do you? I don't think the poor helpless rabbit asked permission to be prey to the hound. The buck to the thirty-aught-six."

"No."

Her father was a great hunter. She had it in for deer rifles. She'd busted three of his up with a sledge hammer, she told him.

"Sex is all we have, Peter. And for me, *ideas* about sex. Notice how I negotiate all my seminar papers into that topic?"

Yes, of course. He was well aware of it.

She was heavy on Freud and on various what she called sexual pleasure magazines. Porn, he told her.

"It's all in your definition," she told him.

He put off Francis Bacon for an hour. He gave her his all— what was left.

"You know," she said, lounging afterwards, "*you*, not me, are stretched between two poles: abstractions and the lust of the flesh. Me, I'm different. It's all of one piece for me. One is an expression of the other. But you—you're a man of wild swings!"

He mused on this.

"Fusion versus fission," she said.

PART TWO

THE GRAND PROJECT

1

News item: "The Finger, now 2,000 feet high, nears completion. On Friday, several hundred devotees gathered around the construction site. One young woman gushed: 'I think it's so cool.' Yet she went on to say: 'Still, I'm not sure why they're picking on the rich. There's a lot of people that ain't rich that I'd like to give the finger to. And have. No rich guy's done anything to me yet. Maybe if he, or she, done it, I'd be singing a different tune.'"

News item: "The man behind the Finger spoke yesterday at a rally of over a thousand people: 'I've no gripe with *all* rich people, don't get me wrong. Just most of them. They don't care about me, you, or the other guy. Just about themselves. After all, how'd they get so rich? That's my position. Give a little of it away, willya?' When asked about the funding for the project, Mr. Finger, as he's become known, said: 'It's still coming in. Over fifty million now from supporters all over the globe. And a heavy helping of free labor!'"

News item: "Mr. Porter Danville, aka the Rich Man, has launched a nuisance suit against Mr. William Stevens, aka Mr. Finger. Mr. Danville explained: 'I can't stand to see that thing rising up out of the earth because I know exactly what's intended by it, and this is obscene and insulting, and I can't stand by silently to watch it grow bigger and bigger with each passing day.'"

News item: "Thousands are mounting a campaign to stop nuisance suits. Small demonstrations in front of the Finger are occurring as well as all-night candlelight vigils."

He had discovered his icon.

He had indeed discovered it—thanks to Bob.

This ground the abstract in the concrete.

This captured Flight or Fight.

Publish or perish. He wouldn't perish now.

He'd been called into Dean Chasm's office the previous semester—about publication. About his *lack* of publication, that is.

"Professor Boatz, please sit down. Please."

It was a hard oak chair to one side of the Dean's desk. The Dean had his long legs extended, and he leaned back easefully in his swivel chair.

Peter sat uncomfortably on the hard oak chair.

"Professor Boatz, this is merely an informative chat. Can I get you anything?"

Peter looked about.

"Coffee?"

"Yes." He perked up at the thought.

"How do you like that coffee?"

"Cream, please."

"Cream. Good, very good."

The Dean poured two cups of coffee. He stirred cream in a white cup and handed it carefully to Peter, balancing it in the air. His hand shook slightly.

"Thanks."

"Now, then . . . now then," the Dean said, once they were both sipping, "the Committee on Publications met of recent date, and it has come to our attention that you have not published anything, sir. For a long period . . . or, rather, to be more exact: never. Isn't that correct—or is something in the works, something the Committee should know about?"

Peter took too large a sip, the hot, creamy coffee pooling in his mouth. He sputtered out: "I'm in the middle of a project . . . presently. I'm presently in the midst of a project."

"Oh, good, very good. Can you please describe that project? What is the book—I assume it's a book—about, specifically?" The Dean grabbed a yellow legal pad. He held a ballpoint poised over it.

"Icons of power."

"Icons of power. Ah, good. Can you give me a completion date? So I can pass this on to the Committee?"

Peter nodded. "Yes, certainly. Certainly I can do that. End of the summer. All will be wrapped up by the end of the summer."

"Good, very good! Publisher? Have you made plans, overtures, sent signals?"

"Uh, none yet. But I'll be seeking one soon—I'm sure, very soon."

The Dean looked long at him. An incipient smile worked on his thick red lips. "Ah," he said. "Well, now. We all have it in us to do good work. Don't we, Professor? Try and *do*. It's like slingshot action. You pull back, then release. Try and do. And there's no question that a willing spirit is invariably rewarded with the prize."

"Thank you," said Peter, "for your support."

"Yes, yes. I'll have very good news for the Committee now." Dean Chasm rose.

He cranked Peter's hand several times before Peter exited the office.

Mornings Peter spent in his cramped office situated in a three-story ancient brick building, with windows you could raise and lower. He'd pulled his desk up to the window to allow a view of several walnut trees on the shadowy grounds of the leafy campus. It was a delightful respite from reading, writing, and thinking.

The shadows of the trees played on the sunlit sidewalk.

He feared interruptions from students. He kept his door closed, locked.

I have a focus now, he thought. *Thanks to Bob.*

He was framing a study.

Suddenly the phone rang.

"Peter, it's Sheila. Oh, Peter, I do hope you aren't too angry with me."

"Angry?"

Damn, he thought, *but she does have a lovely voice.*

"Are you?"

"No, I'm not angry. Why would I be angry?"

"We didn't have much of a visit, did we? And it was all my fault."

"No. It was fine." He recalled the crimson glow in her cheeks. Yes, how blood-flushed they were.

"I'm in town."

"What?"

"I'm in town. Do you want to see me?"

"Yes. Of course."

Still that female power to compel?

He felt vacuum-sucked out of his office, his work.

An hour later he met her in the flesh. They met at a bar.

"I was just so awful to you," Sheila said, stroking his hands. "But half of it was teasing. It was just a bunch of teasing, Peter. And I thought you'd see it, but you didn't!" The deafening, cacophonous music in the bar drowned out half of what she was saying, but Peter gathered it was basically along these lines: Her marriage was over. She wanted some sort of life. *They'd* had one—hadn't they? She wanted things back the way they'd been before—way back when. Yes, admittedly, those times could have been *better*. But they were good, like he'd said. She was just sore—sore for him leaving her the way he did. Not being faithful—not sticking to it. But she wanted to put all that behind them.

"Move on," she said. "Don't you think?"

She continued to stroke his hand.

He was buzzed.

"Speak," she said. "Speak to me of your feelings. Please tell me, Peter. I know you still have them. I saw it. I felt it—ever so much!"

She was heavy with perfume.

"What is that you're wearing?" he asked. He sniffed.

"Pomegranate. The choice of perfumes, honey." Her hand moved up his arm. Her mouth serenaded him with the possibilities: Couldn't they, if they tried real hard, resurrect that past? What if two people thought they could, couldn't they?

He tried to resist, but she had him in her sights. That odiferous pomegranate.

"Maybe, maybe . . . if things were mutually agreed on."

She spoke of how it would go. She'd become a realist over those fifteen long years—a hardcore realist. She'd gotten tough. "I'm a tough woman. A professional woman. I understand things better," she said. "A whole lot better." She stared at him, expectantly.

"Oh, good," he said.

She nodded. She understood the path ahead of her, of him too, much better now. Before, it had only been Sex and Babies. That was all she could see. "Remember?" she said.

"Yes," he said.

"But now I've got the whole picture. The whole shooting match."

He took a quick drink with his free hand.

Now, she said, *now,* she could see the whole Life Cycle of the Average Person—oh, it was so clear to her, whereas before, *somehow*—who could explain it?—she hadn't even noticed it. Not really. Not that she didn't *know* it—everyone *knew* it, but knowing and noticing were two very different things. You knew plenty of things you didn't exactly take notice of. Wasn't that true?

"True," he said.

"Am I being clear?"

"Sure."

"You're the professor." She gripped his arm. "I'm so glad you think so." She went on, now drumming his arm: If he would but join her before it was too late—join with her to make a Perfect Life. Well, at least, as perfect as one could get it. Really, she was thinking of *his* welfare as much as her own, wanting him not to waste any more of *his* life—please, she said, just *do* this. Just consider, as to what doth yet remain—

"Doth?" he said.

"Figure of speech." She went on: Sex, Babies, Rearing, Aging, Death, Burial. And, of course, concurrently with all that: Job or Career. "Where are we, the two of *us,* on this continuum? We're, both of us, stuck with the *last,* Peter. Job, career—but is that enough? Is it? Really, it's so abundantly obvious, isn't it? We're not even at Sex and Babies yet! My husband—oh, I hate to even call him my husband—he refused to give me Babies. You know what? He got a vasectomy right off the bat?—right off the bat, Peter! Can you believe it? And he didn't even tell me! I found it out later! That horrible bastard! But that's another story, and not one I'm particularly given to repeating. The point is, I still want Babies. Sex is getting on the train, Peter, but Babies follow like all the cars and the caboose."

47

"By train, you mean the engine?"

"Yes, the engine."

"But there's the rest of it, isn't there—regardless?" he said.

She gripped his arms hard, her fingernails digging in. "You and me? We've got maybe forty years, fifty tops, before we're stuck in the frigging ground!"

"God!" he said. He yelped at her fingernails. She let go.

He examined the marks.

"You're okay. I was just steamed up," she said. "I often get that way: At the *prospect* of *only* the aging, the death, the burial. Don't you see?"

"It's the lot man was born for."

"Quit it!"

She asked him what he was doing this summer.

She can't, he thought. *She just can't.* And yet . . . She leaned forward and the odiferous pomegranate engulfed him entirely. "A book . . . I'm writing a book."

"Figures. What's it about?"

He hesitated.

"Now, come on," she said. "I won't bite."

He still hesitated.

"Are you going to tell me or not?" she said. And then she moved closer and fingered his chest. "You poor thing. Afraid to tell your sweet little Shelia."

He launched out. And once he'd launched out, he couldn't seem to restrain himself. Perhaps it was sheer atavism—his Pub self reemerging—that propelled him wildly on. An academic work, he rhapsodized: political, philosophical, psychological—mythical! Did she recall that Finger business her friend Bob brought up? A central icon, that Finger was, embodying class struggle throughout the centuries in one visible, shocking image. The very essence of nemesis. But more—much more: the perfect concretized abstraction—

He saw her displeasure mounting.

He gulped his drink.

"Bob—he's such a bore. Why waste your time on such as that?"

"Publish or perish," said Peter.

"What all have you published?"

"The Finger," he said. "It will make up . . . for everything."

"Look at all the waste already on that Finger," she said.

"How so?"

"All the money that could be directed elsewhere, to hospitals, to food production, to education, to the space program."

"Perhaps you have a point," he said.

"How many new houses would that build? How much baby food?"

"Definitely a point," he said.

"Have you thought about that?"

Millions, he said, had thrown only one to ten dollars toward it.

"People shouldn't complain. They should take what they're given and make the best of it. Make lemonade. That's my philosophy." She went on to say how she'd mapped her whole life out—did he want to hear? Did he want to see?

He ordered refills.

She'd written it all down. How everything was to go: every year, every month, every single day for the upcoming year.

"Enterprising."

"For instance, this week I'm *here*. Next week, I know exactly where I'll be if you don't make a decision that pleases me. I do have alternate plans, Peter, given that in one scenario you're part of it, and in the other, you're not. But if you're not *in* it, I go on to Plan B, Man Two. I'm not as attracted to him as I am to you, but I'll have to settle. Do your best, but be ready to settle. I'm visionary but practical."

"Interesting," he noted.

"It's the professional woman in me coming out."

And then she produced a calendar.

She raised a finger. If he gave her the go-ahead today, she'd go shopping first thing tomorrow—for a wedding dress. She'd be up by six, breakfast at seven, and be out and about by eight. "Let's call it the Event," she said. "I've got the day marked out, hour by hour. Now I wouldn't want you to be *with* me because frankly you'd slow me down." She laid out what each day would be like, and when the wedding would need to occur. "Maybe I sound like I'm in a rush," she said. "Well, I *am*. I'm thirty-five years old, Peter, and I don't have any more time to waste. My child bearing years will soon come to an abrupt halt! You've got three days"—she showed him on the calendar—"to make up your mind, or it's Plan B."

"Man Two."

"That's correct."

"Three days?"

"That's adequate. That's sufficient."

She said it was now time to mention all the things she wanted in her life—she had lists, well-organized. She produced a black folder. She directed him along: the kind of house, the kind of furniture, the kind of dishes, the kind of silverware, accent pieces, rugs, books, computers, TVs. You weren't *grounded* in life at all unless you had specific things to ground you. "You think about it," she said, applying lipstick, "if you don't have a lot of things, you are less real somehow. I'm not ready to ascend into the spiritual sphere as yet. But that's what happens when you shed your flesh and *rise up there*!" She pointed up at the rough hewn cedar ceiling beams. "I ask you: Do the ghostly, the disembodied, do they possess earthly things? I think not. Things make you alive and breathing!"

"I have very few things," he noted.

"Then you won't crowd our house." She leaned toward him and placed one hand on each shoulder. "*Thinginess*," she said. "Are you familiar?" Her fingernails dug in a little. "I think of that bare room of yours back in college. It was like you were about to bid goodbye to the planet!" She let up and her hands fell to his arms. She said thinginess was like weights that gave you ballast, kept you from soaring. She spoke of her investor husband, with his computer bleeps on the screen—were those *real* in any sense of the word? She spoke of how he was always erasing real things from their mutual existence like you'd sweep dust out of your house. All those trips to the Goodwill. Sure, you had to reduce clutter, but so many things he'd gotten rid of had her *life* stamped on them. "My life was *in* those things," she said. She removed her hands from him. "It was like he was killing me off bit by bit. He was taking away a certain memory, a certain smell, a certain way this or that thing felt, or made me feel—happy or sad."

That odiferous pomegranate—he swooned.

He invited her to his apartment.

"No, no. None of *that* until a commitment is made. I feel so driven, Peter. Each hour ticking away, ticking, ticking, ticking! Fifteen years wasted, utterly wasted!"

"Make lemonade," he said.

"I *am* making lemonade! But that doesn't change the fact that I've got to make the best of it. And I am trying to do that. Each minute, Peter. We live by minutes, seconds, nanoseconds. Each is a measure of our blood coursing through our veins and arteries. Time is running out for each and every one of us. Me—you, Peter! Clicking off, clicking off!"

Here was a desperate woman, he thought. The jock in him put him on the prowl.

"But you're not old. And you're very attractive." He grasped her hand.

"You have but one thing in mind," she said, pulling loose. "But no thank you. Still, my physical appearance belies the truth. In my case, the aging, Peter, is *inside*—not outside."

"Isn't our skin but an outward sign of an inward condition?"

"You're so sweet."

"If you'd let me be."

"I'm a great reader of the connections between spirit and flesh," she said. "The flesh has first priority. Until that moment, you see, until that *time* . . ."

"That departure?"

"Yes. Oh, god, Peter. I just *hate* my calendar, but it was an absolute must." She folded her hands. "God, sometimes when I think about it all—"

"But you're so young," he said.

"Cut the bullshit! Flesh," she said. "Flesh, Peter."

He returned to his apartment, a four-story brick French style fronting a narrow brick street. For a spell, he had in mind that ultimatum of Sheila's. And then he put it out of his mind. No, he thought. No. As mesmerizing as she could be . . . the answer must be no.

A serene evening breeze blew in through the open window. He returned to his project. He'd lost some steam. Onward, he thought. Forge ahead, now.

2

Assistant Dean Lucinda Marigold called. Could Peter teach a late-scheduled summer seminar?

He cringed. "What class would it be?"

"An afternoon class in Modernist, Contemporary, and Futurist Icons. We have some interest."

"How many students?"

"Five. But we'll pay a full load since it's summer, and these students need this course."

"What time?"

"Three-thirty to six Monday/Wednesday. Starts tomorrow..."

"*Tomorrow*?"

"Yes, I'm afraid so. Sorry for the late notice."

"Well ..."

"You're not wanting this exactly, are you?"

He was quite occupied at present, he confessed—but, well, he guessed he could do it.

"Good. Wonderful. Drop by my office in an hour and pick up the student profiles."

Assistant Dean Marigold was new to the administration, hired the previous spring semester. A rather attractive woman, he thought. He saw a quick wit in her brown, lively eyes. He judged her to be, like him, in her mid-thirties.

Her small office was to the right side of the administrative space, as one entered—Dean Chasm's to the left. He could see Dean Chasm looking up vacantly at him from across the space. Or was he even looking at him? Perhaps he was gazing at nothing in particular.

Assistant Dean Marigold handed him the packet.

"With one exception, these are students who are *not* in the Icon Program," she said. "They're crossovers from other programs, and they're planning on taking just this one course. Judging from their letters, I take it they're not all that *interested* in taking your course, but their graduate programs have recently required this, starting in the fall, that is. They want to get a jump on it. As you'll see in the letters."

"One exception?"

"Yes—Mercy Merry. You've had her before, it seems. Her letter is . . . well, there's no other way to put it: It's an outrage." She gave him a quick smile.

Yes, he thought. He would have predicted it.

"Have a good class."

He watched her mouth move. There was such a delicate movement of lips. She might have been savoring ice cream.

Mercy Merry, a red-haired engine of destruction—ill-tempered, utterly inflammatory, challenging everything he said, yet bright, as bright as they came. And a real looker—he couldn't help but note it. What delicate feminine features! What lusty curves! Halfway finished with her Ph.D. in Iconic Studies, she was refusing any iconography that made even the slightest reference to gender or sexuality. When he'd held his night class in a bar—where most of his classes eventually gravitated to—she shook her draught beer at him, wildly expostulating on how it was impossible for him or *any* man to think of women in any other way than the sexual.

"What specifically did I say?" he asked.

He feared she'd accuse him of a leer. There might be a case, he mused.

Two students came forward, defending him, demanding examples.

Boot lickers? He hoped not.

"The subtext," she said.

"But even so, let's say I *had* made an *oblique* reference to the sexual—or even *mentioned* it—isn't that part of life?"

"Do you think of men in the sexual?"

"You just said *men*," he pointed out. "Gender?"

"I was operating within *your* duality," she said. "It wasn't mine."

He spoke of Mother Teresa. *Mother.*

"You don't have to know her *gender*," snapped Mercy Merry. "That is irrelevant."

"You just said *her,*" said Peter.

"Again," she said, "*your* duality. It isn't rocket science. Besides, this whole thing bores the hell out of me. We've been over it and over it. Why bore ourselves further?"

"Yes, why?" he said.

"You started it," she said.

But had he? She often said *you started it.* But then he'd try to think back. Had he?

He opened the packet—Mercy Merry's letter first. Her argument was threefold:

1. I will do minimal work in the Modernist Period—disputing any and all icons. I don't really believe in icons. I see my role as a necessary thorn.

2. I will give most of my attention to the Contemporary—my own period. The past is of little use to me. Tell me what the Past *is,* exactly.

3. I will give no attention to the Future. What does that mean anyway? Where *is* the Future? Give me the coordinates. Latitude and longitude, please.

This would mean, Peter thought, turning this prospect over in his mind, a "C" at best. But of course he could not give *Mercy Merry* a "C." Suicidal. Work out a "B." But then, that would be problematic as well. How could you give Mercy Merry a "B"? You would not dare give this woman a "B." No, it would have to be an "A minus." And, at his university, an A minus was turned in as an "A."

But what about the other four students? He'd have to give them an "A" too, wouldn't he? Of course if he met with them in a bar, that meant "A's" all around.

"The hell with them!" he cried. He slung the packet down. "The hell with them! Give them all an 'A'!"

3

It was important to arrive a bit early to make some coffee, settle in, and not have to be barraged by the students as soon as you entered the room. He got there a half hour before class took up. The students started filing in fifteen minutes later. There were two, then three, then four. They stood at the coffee pot, filling their cups.

Five minutes into introductions, Mercy Merry rocketed in.

"God, I'm sorry! I got held up in traffic."

"Held up?" said Bill Parsely.

"Yes—held up, detained, derailed." She slammed her book bag on the table, and then picked it up and set it on the floor. "I'm sorry, Professor Boatz. I did not intend to be late."

"That's certainly understandable," said Peter. "Certainly understandable." He handed her a syllabus.

She scanned it as he remade introductions. "This is Bill Parsely. Miles Martin. Joyce Early. Ted Bowerhunt. Mercy Merry."

"And now we all know each other," said Bill Parsely.

A wiseacre. Trouble.

The bar, though—next meeting. The bar would put a buzz in all of them, and one need not worry. Let the students run the class. Let them expostulate and equivocate all they wanted. He could drink beer and listen in.

"Now then," he said. He covered the general parameters of the course: Modernist Icons (not castles, but skyscrapers; not robes but suits); Contemporary Icons (not suits but casual wear; not skyscrapers, but underground spaces reportedly inhabited by the military and aliens), the Futurist Icons—

"I don't get it. I'm sorry to interrupt, but I just don't understand *why* these are icons." He had not expected trouble from this mousy looking little woman—Joyce Early. But this confusion, sure, he must address it.

"It's all in the definitions," he said. "It's my own iconography. The way I see it. Not all would, of course." He knew what was coming. But he was, after all, the professor.

"*Why* do you see it that way?" said Mercy Merry. She was biting her ballpoint pen. She always bit her ballpoints. They had bite marks halfway down the shaft.

"Ah," he said. "We've been over this before. Haven't we?"

"Not with *them*."

"These things can be seen from multiple perspectives," said Peter. "I grant you that. A ballpoint, such as you have there—"

She withdrew it from her mouth, then reinserted it.

"That's a Modernist Icon, isn't it? It meant not having to dip the ink pen nib into the well, and before that not having to dip the feather—"

"But," said Bill Parsely, "technology. That's all it is. You spoke of the cross in your syllabus. There, sir, *is* an icon. But a ballpoint pen is not a cross."

He looked around with a grin that searched for supporters. Joyce Early was not amused. But Miles Martin moved his cup a tad forward on the conference table. "I'd like to interject," he said. "If you don't mind."

"I don't mind."

"The cross, as seen, isn't an icon either."

"Oh?" said Peter.

"The cross we see isn't the original cross. This cross is a consumer *image* of the *real* cross. You can buy it in chocolate flavor. You can purchase it in greeting cards."

"You miss it," said Mercy Merry. "You miss it." And she withdrew the tooth-bitten ballpoint from her mouth and pointed it at the lot of them.

"How did we miss it?" asked Joyce. She looked hurt.

"Well, I didn't say *you* missed it," said Mercy. "Don't be so touchy. But anyone who doesn't understand that the cross itself *isn't* an icon, I mean the *real* cross, is missing it. How is the cross, the *real* cross, an icon?"

He would leave it to them to battle this one out.

Ted Bowerhunt shook his head and looked off in space. "Is there a *real* cross to begin with?"

"That's my meaning!" said Mercy. "Is there a *real* cross? What's real about it? Even if you touched it, set it right here before me, what's *real* about it? What do you *mean* by real?"

"Sure, there is a real cross," said Joyce. "Of course, there is a real cross."

"Real in what sense?"

"Real in a lot of senses."

"Name one."

Joyce Early's lips trembled. "I don't know how to say this without sounding over-religious or something, but it's real to those who *believe* in it."

"So an icon is real to those who believe in it."

"Yes."

"Do you believe it's snowing? Take a look."

"No. It's not snowing."

"And yet I tell you I believe that it *is* snowing. And so that snow, for me, is an icon. It's an icon of wondrous relief from this awful heat." She reinserted the ballpoint.

"It's not hot in *this* room, at least," observed Ted Bowerhunt. "What is the thermostat set for—fifty?"

"We'll see about that," said Peter. "I'll check with maintenance."

"It depends on how you define icon," said Ted Bowerhunt.

"It depends on a lot of things," said Miles Martin.

"It depends on nothing," said Mercy Merry.

"What do you mean?" said Joyce Early.

"*Nothing*. Something. I'm sorry, *something*."

"What?" said Joyce. "Which something?"

"That's it, isn't it? *Which* something? Which is it?"

"We are getting nowhere," said Ted Bowerhunt. He turned to Peter. "Aren't you supposed to be teaching us something?"

"Which *something*?" said Mercy Merry. "Which something is he supposed to be teaching us?"

"What *are* you, exactly?" asked Joyce.

"Me? I'm nothing," said Mercy Merry.

Miles Martin laughed. "Oh, you're something all right?"

Mercy Merry gave him a long, hard look, but then one of

amusement. "What does that mean—what's your name?"

"Miles. Miles Martin?"

"How am I to read that comment?"

"Read it as you wish."

"*Ah*, I like that."

Joyce cleared her throat. Twice. "Do you all know something I don't? Is there something I missed out on? Because frankly, I don't understand what's going on."

"Nothing," said Ted Bowerhunt. "Nothing at all."

"Then, please," said Joyce, "I'd like to hear what the professor has to say." She looked directly at Peter.

"Why don't we adjourn to a fine bar I know in town," said Peter.

4

"You live in this city, and you don't even know about this theme park?"

"No."

"Strange. Odd," she said.

"It's a real winner, is it?"

"A blessed event to me—I discovered it in the tail end of my marriage to that horrible Investor Man. I was looking around, you see—I was desperately *needing, seeking.*"

"Oh."

"You must comprehend," she said, instructing him with her finger, "what is meant by *thinginess*—an object lesson. Call me a materialist," she said, "if you will. Call me a hoarder if you will. But are they identical with thinginess? I hate equivocation," she said. "Get on the interstate."

They came to it. Eventually.

She jabbered it up all the way.

He grew weary of it—her nonstop lecture on *thinginess.* Its many ins and outs. His mind grew numb.

But now here they were.

Across from a WORLDS OF DELIGHT & GRANDIOSE ADVENTURE!

LIVING YOUR LIFE THEME PARK

At the Gate, an attendant in a booth accepted Peter's credit card.

They drove in.

"Two hundred! That's pretty stiff."

"Pretty nominal for what you get," said Sheila. "Drive to Building 1." She pointed to the east. It was some distance away, bright red, the first of a string of interconnected buildings.

"You really didn't know about this place?"

"No."

"All of my ideas," she said, "come from this place—and their literature. You know what they call it? Their huge tome of ideas and things?"

"No. What?"

"*A Compendium of Thinginess.* See over there? Stop right up there."

He parked in front of a two-story brick building with an enormous sign in front. On this sign were pictured a man and woman each about to bite into two halves of a juicy bright red apple. Their faces were conjoined in ecstatic, anticipatory enjoyment.

"Paired pieces," said Shelia. "Half his, half hers. A symbolic act of eating, consuming. I just love it!"

"Sharing an apple."

"That's what lovers do, silly."

"I suppose they explain that in the literature," he said.

"Yes, they do. And the *Compendium* is stored in that very building. Of course, you can get it as an e-book." She patted his hand. "On to Building 1."

There was something of a traffic jam there. Plus, a few hundred people were herding from their cars to the building.

"Droves," muttered Sheila.

They parked way out.

Even from there, one couldn't miss the flashy, lurid red sign on Building 1 announcing in dancing digital: "It Starts Here—Sex!"

When he opened the car door, Sheila grabbed his hand. "Wait a minute, honey. Shut the door. Please."

He did as she bid.

She looked at him closely, intimately.

"Before we go in. Okay?"

"Yes?"

"You need to know."

"What?"

"I spotted this place on the Internet a year ago, and I've read all their literature. Studied it, *consumed* it—stored it up right here." She thrust a finger at her heart. "It's given me such a new handle on things, Peter. Such a new vision. See, it's a stage-by-stage thing. Just like I've been telling you: Life's stages. And it's right here in your own city, and you didn't know a thing about it—you the Icon Man!"

"You can't know everything," he said.

"Some things you should know. And know *this*, I take this stuff seriously—okay? So don't mock."

"I won't."

"Good."

They joined a few hundred people herding into the lurid red Building 1.

It smelled strongly of some odor. Was it . . .

"Pomegranate," said Peter. "I smell pomegranate."

"Sure you do. They sell it in the Compendium Building. It's very sexual. Don't you think?"

They could hardly budge in the busy, heaving throng crowding The Facts of Sex exhibit.

"Push," shouted Sheila. "You have to *push*."

It was a solid assemblage of human bodies pulsing, pushing, pressing, and swaying.

One sensed a tremendous urgency.

"Push. You're the big jock!" yelled Sheila. "Push, damn it! Make a hole!"

Eventually, inching their way, they shoved their way to the front.

"Look at that—just look at that!" whispered Sheila, taking Peter's hand in her moist palm.

She signaled the graphic displays of sexual foreplay and innumerable coital positions.

"Speak of public displays of affection," said Peter.

"It all starts here," said Sheila, solemnly. She gripped his hand.

"But how do you—"

"How *do* you?" said Sheila.

"How?" said Peter.

"Porn? You think it's porn? Is that what you think?"

"Indeed not. Basic biology," said Peter.

An aging woman pushed her way in. She directed a busy finger at the display. "Let me speak to that. It's normal. It's unequivocally normal. You tell me if everyone hasn't, huh? Hasn't everyone?"

A young man moved into the fold. "Sure they have." He sighed. "What'd you expect? The stork?"

The aging woman combed back a strand of gray hair. "You know about this, do you? You look a bit wet behind the ears."

"I'm twenty-one."

"I'd never guessed."

"Well, I am."

"*Thinginess*," pronounced Sheila. "Isn't that what it is?"

"Indeed it is. Don't you just love the *Compendium*?"

"My cup of tea," said Sheila.

"My husband says it beats the Bible, all that *he knew her* stuff, but I tell him, look, it's all the same. It amounts to the same thing."

Bodies were pressing, pushing, bumping from behind.

They moved on.

They wormed their way through the crowded Contraception Display. "No!" shrieked Sheila. "Not me! Not us! No!"

They burrowed through the throng to Pregnancy.

"*This*," Sheila said, "is what *you* need to pay attention to." She clenched Peter's hand. "This—this is what *you* want to avoid. Well, not with me you won't!"

Here there was considerably less human traffic. They faced the exhibit: sperm, egg, zygote, embryo, developing fetus, amniotic fluid.

"It's a whole little life in there," said Sheila, her voice hushed. "You know what the *Compendium* says?"

"No. What?"

"Life is shot into being—at both ends."

"Really?"

"That shot—into the World. Isn't that beautiful? Isn't that *so* beautiful? To be shot into the World?"

"Well, I don't know."

"You know what the *Compendium* says?"

"No."

"That's *real* thinginess. You can't know thinginess until you experience *Baby*. And I believe that."

"Are you sure?"

"In Baby, you revisit *you* as Baby. You come full circle."

"Oh."

"But see, you, Peter, don't know thinginess at all. Do you?"

"Not at all? Never make too bold a generalization," he said, a professorial axiom he lived by. "Allow for the exception."

"You know what that first shot is?"

"Of course."

"I doubt it."

"What, then?"

"It's the launch. Life is violent, Peter. Life is an explosion. Think sperm. I'll bet you think fluid or *juice*. Is *sperm* fluid or juice?"

"No."

No pressing, pushing, pulsating flesh here. They could stand here as long as they wished. Onlookers came and went. Not Sheila.

"What *is* sperm?"

"A thing?" he said.

"*It knows not*," said Sheila. "I quote the *Compendium*—if you'll allow me."

"An authoritative source?"

"Don't make fun—please. I hold it in high regard. I reverence it."

"If it knows *not*, what does it *not* know?"

"Itself. You. Anything. Nothing. It's sheer thing. It's thinginess itself—in miniature. That's what the *Compendium* says. *It knows not.* You'd have to read the Philosophy Section to know these things, honey. I'd think a professor like you would love the *Compendium's* Philosophy Section."

"How long is it?"

"Hundreds of pages. Thousands. I can't believe you don't know about it. You know what?"

"What?"

"It's being incorporated into many, many college classes."

"Oh."

"I read it every day. I read and memorize it. Like Bible verses. You know how people do that. The *Compendium*—it's my Bible. It's philosophy, but it's more than that. It's useful."

"I wouldn't have guessed," said Peter.

"Don't mock! You don't have to love it, but you can at least not mock."

She pulled him by the hand, her fingernails digging in. "Okay, now we move on. You're so interested in Baby-making. You've had your fill, haven't you?"

They took in the rest: Childbirth, Rearing, Young Adulthood, Adulthood, Aging

Death, Burial.

It was all so—full, yes, of *thinginess*. At every stage, nourishment of the flesh—food and water. Nutrition. Growth. Flesh's incessant need for continuance, its resistance to incipient decay.

In the Aging Building, a gray sign read: "Decay is Manifest in Every Cell."

In the Burial Building, Sheila grew morose. "I just feel so, so sad here. To think . . . to think it all has to end like this. Why should it? What's the point? Really, can you tell me, Peter, what's the point? You're some big professor. What is it?"

"Does there have to be a point?"

"There sure isn't any—at least to my way of thinking."

When they exited the Burial building, it was night. Bouncy jazz music filled the air. Cars and trucks spun in the gravel lot. Engines snarled.

From here you could see the raunchy, riotous multicolored light works display of WORLDS OF DELIGHT & GRANDIOSE ADVENTURE! The interstate traffic hummed along, lit up like multitudinous fireflies.

"Onto the Compendium Building," said Sheila.

"Oh, no. I can't. I'm too tired."

"Peter. You *must* see the Compendium Building. They sell *everything*. And a person *should* buy everything here because it's all matched and color coordinated. Cribs to caskets!"

"My god. That's in their literature—is it? That last? Cribs to—"

"Yes, yes—of course it is. Why wouldn't it be?"

They entered the Compendium Display Room.

A few people hung around a multivolume tome, spread out like an auto repair manual on an extremely long table. Peter judged the table to be about twenty feet long.

"The *Compendium*," said Sheila. Her voice became soft, worshipful. "Isn't it... just lovely looking? Isn't it... just magnificent to behold?"

"And so you've mastered it all?"

"Some of it. It would take years, of course."

"I thought you said—"

"Don't be so literal. *Please.*"

They gravitated to the Life's Needs Section.

The entrance was blocked.

Bodies wall to wall. Breaths. Exhalations. Wheezes. Burps. Coughs.

"You have to *assert* yourself," she said. "Like before. You'll never, ever make a deal if you don't."

"Make a deal?"

"*Buy. Purchase. Acquire.* Come on."

She clenched her credit card.

At six-two, he could see over heads. Credit cards held poised in hands. The comforts of the body all on sale: lotions, soaps, perfumes, beds, covers, sheets, pillows, home furnishings, houses, cars, sailboats.

A man with a microphone boomed out: "We've got it. Everything you *need* and *want.* If it's not right here, ladies and gents, you can order it. All sales are final."

He yelled it again like a circus barker.

"Move in. Move *in*," urged Sheila.

When they exited the building, Sheila clutched three large packages.

"I feel so *dizzy.* I'm half dead, Peter. Weary. Worn. All those hideous *creatures*—being up against them like that. Smelling them. Up against their ugly faces—pitted skin, growths, pustules. What a bunch of mangy animals! I'm agoraphobic. Did I ever mention it?"

"No."

"I am. In grocery stores too!"

"What about thinginess?"

"What about it?"

"Wasn't that thinginess—all those human bodies?"

"Sure."

"Your fellow man," said Peter. "His wants, needs—the stiff whiff of mortality?"

She grimaced. "Three days," she said, rubbing her hands together. "Give me your answer. Now."

"No."

"No?"

"Not yet."

"Well, then. Soon. It had better be *soon*. And I mean it!"

5

He was sitting in the Faculty Club when Assistant Dean Marigold spotted him.

He held his pen, poised.

"Ah," she said. "How is the class?"

"Fine. Rich. Fertile."

"Ah. Good." She looked down at his composition book. "I see you keep a journal. A wonderful habit, that is."

"Oh, it's not exactly a journal—"

"It looks like a journal."

"It's book ideas."

"Book? Wonderful."

"Research. Mostly."

"Of course. What's it about? If you don't mind my asking."

"Icons."

"Of course. I would have predicted this. Which icons?"

He smoothed out the pages. "Power. The vestages of power. Feudal to contemporary. Money, land, property, weaponry, torture, lethal killing machines—and so forth."

"There' s no end?"

"Hard to say."

A finger rubbed her lip. "You will read deeply into each? Where's the *real* meaning located? The center? What *is* an icon? What is a thing only? Who invests it with meaning? Is the investing authentic? Who are the stakeholders? Who respects them *as* stakeholders? Is there an abstract referent that partakes of the eternal? The perfect? The transcendental? Questions such as these?"

"Yes," he said. "Yes, yes."

She smiled, waved, and headed off.

Ah, that Assistant Dean.

"Icons of Power?" said Mercy Merry. "My lord. I suppose these

68

are decided on according to the traditional divisions between class, culture, race, and gender?"

"I don't see how else they could be decided."

"Of course," said Bill Parsely.

"Nothing new."

"I don't know about this," said Joyce Early. "Please. Tell me."

"What's to know?" said Mercy Merry. "And I suppose you have some key totalizing icon?"

"I think so," he said. He attempted to fill them in.

He read from a recent article: "Police surrounded the Finger to keep order as the latest candlelight vigil was disrupted by several protesters with signs that read: 'STOP THE PROJECT! GIVE MR. FINGER THE FINGER!'"

"As you see," said Peter.

"Old news."

"How common."

"Ah, but it *is* different," said Bill Parsely. "You give the finger out of road rage, out of rage of all kinds, but to build a Finger of this size—rebuking the rich—this is worth exploring, whether iconic or not."

"I have passing interest in it," said Mercy Merry.

"I find it horribly revolting," said Joyce Early. "But I guess it *is* an icon. Isn't it?"

6

There was a university-wide party at the new President's mansion. Peter spotted Assistant Dean Marigold and moved toward her with a drink in his hand and a cracker topped with cheese whiz.

"Hello, Professor Boatz." She held out her hand. Her words were slurred.

"Hello."

"Have you met the new President?"

"No—"

"A man with a vision. A man with big ideas."

"Which ideas?"

"His plan for the university. Have you read it?"

"No." He never read such things.

"Grandiose, truly. Corporate liaisons. Industrial liaisons. Military liaisons. Even with your department—as you'll see."

"Icons? Liaisons—with whom?"

"Grocery Kingdom, for one." She finished off her glass. She looked around. "I'm needing—"

"I'll get it," he said.

The Assistant Dean was particularly alluring this evening. An aggressive male impulse seized him like a clenched fist.

"Oh, how very kind of you." Her voice made him think of slippery mud.

"What kind?"

"Pardon? Oh, anything. Anything at all. I'm not particular. As long as it's hard." She smiled. "It's that kind of night."

He moseyed along to the President's cash bar.

Shouldn't the drinks be free? Really, shouldn't they?

He finished his drink off as he waited, then watched the drinks being made, paid, and returned with two crackers with cheese whiz on a plate, and two hard drinks in a drink holder.

She took one of each. "You're so very kind. Not every faculty member is this kind to me."

A man came up and shook Assistant Dean Marigold's hand. The man was soon jabbering on. He was a small, excitable fellow with a tie loose at the collar, and he motioned his glass up and down, the ice clinking. "We're already dealing with it. We're planning carefully. We had a PowerPoint yesterday afternoon—forty of us there—dealing with it. How to create the liaisons. How to work the liaisons. How to energize the liaisons once created. We all left totally in a dither. It wasn't what I would call a productive meeting."

"Oh, it's going to bring monumental change," said the Assistant Dean.

"We've had support personnel threatening to quit."

"Professor Boatz, Professor Walkman."

"Pleased," said Walkman. "And your area is?"

"Icons."

"Icons . . . umm. Yes, of course. I've had students who took your courses. Some happy, some . . . not particularly so. Well, you know."

"Yes," said Peter.

"He's a lion," said the Assistant Dean, pointing toward the man with the massive, leonine head, gray beard, and magnanimous looking gestures. "A Renaissance looking man, isn't he? There you behold him, Peter, President Lance Winger. There he is, your deity."

Winger came out *Whing-your*.

"Goddamn it," said Walkman, "but our department is coming *apart*."

"I wouldn't doubt it," said the Assistant Dean.

Peter drank off his drink.

"And yours?" said Walkman, turning to Peter.

"Not yet."

"Well, you will see soon enough," said Walkman. "Won't he?"

"Grocery Kingdom," said Assistant Dean Marigold. "They took a fetching interest in Professor Boatz's icons."

The Assistant Dean was in no shape to drive.

Peter offered to take her home.

"But what about my car?"

"I'll drive you home in your car."

"Oh—no. No . . ."

"I insist."

"But what about *your* car?"

"I walked."

A lie.

"Oh—god, well okay. You are such a dear." It came out *durr.* He drove her home in her car. She told him to park on the street. He walked her to her door. She stopped, before entering, and gave him a quick kiss. And then, of a sudden, she pulled him closer and kissed him hard. "That's for being such a *durr*," she said.

She opened the door and disappeared inside.

Assistant Dean Lucinda Marigold. He felt the tightness of her body against his. He felt the brush of her soft hair against his neck. He felt those soft, moist lips.

7

He was having coffee in the Faculty Club when Mercy Merry showed up.

"Hello," she said.

"Hello."

"May I sit down?"

"You're not supposed to be here. Are you?"

"Why not?"

"Faculty only."

"Rules," she said. She carried coffee. "I wanted to speak to you."

"About what?"

"About the Finger." She swept a wave of flaming red hair out of her eyes. "It shows great . . . I'm looking for the word . . . great openness. To new iconic values. There I've said it."

"That wasn't so hard, was it?"

"You're not stuck in the Middle Ages, and that's . . . so good. You're not stuck in Ancient Greece or Rome. You're not stuck in the Great War." She looked about. "I need dessert."

"I'll buy," he said.

"Cocoanut cream pie," she said. "My favorite."

Peter went for it. He got one himself.

They were average size pieces.

A fellow professor was now lodged, leaning at his table speaking to Mercy Merry.

"Oh," she was saying, "well, thank you. I didn't think it was all that good. You say *standard*. Which standard exactly—if you don't mind my asking?"

It was Professor Batch, a fellow Icon professor, shaped like a bowling pin, large in the buttocks, small in the chest. "The same standard as usual: clarity."

"How was mine clear?" she asked.

"It wasn't unclear," he said.

"Then by clear, you simply mean *not unclear*."

"That's what I mean exactly," he said. He stuck his pipe in his mouth, and then suddenly retracted it. "Oh, hello, Peter." He sat down.

Peter slid the coconut cream pie to Mercy Merry.

"Oh, thank you, thank you," she said.

"Just a minute," said Professor Batch. "Don't eat."

"What?" said Mercy Merry.

"Look at the shape of those two pieces," said Professor Batch. "Notice. May I?"

"Well, all right," said Mercy Merry. "If you must."

He grabbed her coconut cream pie and placed it next to Peter's.

"Notice," he said, pointing a finger, "how this one's edge meets the other one's edge."

"So?"

"Companion pieces," said Professor Batch. "These could be put back together. Though it would be difficult to arrange this. How, once you cut one thing apart from another, can you reassemble them? Can they ever be reassembled? Only in our minds—isn't that correct?"

He slid the coconut cream pie back to Mercy Merry.

"And so?" said Mercy Merry.

"There's a conundrum for you. Can it ever be done?"

"Preservationists can deal with tiny threads of paper," said Peter.

"But cut edges of pie or filling?"

Mercy Merry ate. "What's the status of the question?"

"Everything is so imperfect," said Professor Batch.

"What's perfect?"

"I wouldn't mind a piece myself," said Professor Batch.

"Then get yourself one," said Mercy Merry.

"I'm working on your previous," said Professor Batch. "Clear means *not unclear*. I've never thought of it that way. But that makes perfect sense."

"Sure it does. If we accept that there is a 'perfect sense' to begin with. But, for now, what's *not unclear*?"

Peter forked a piece of pie into his mouth.

Professor Batch was eyeing the delivery. "What would you say, Peter?" he asked. "How do we define *not unclear*?"

"Clear."

"But what about unclear?"

"Not clear."

"What exactly is clear?" asked Mercy Merry.

"Many things are clear," said Peter. "Many things are not."

"That's a good point," said Professor Batch.

"The things that are very clear," said Peter, "are utterly without obfuscation. Think of a window without dirt, dust, smudges, bug stains . . . we say that window is *clean*. We don't say it's clear, but it's a useful parallel for an idea that is without dirt, dust, smudges, and bug stains. If you see what I mean."

"But you've defined it in the negative," said Professor Batch. "As not being . . . well, essentially dirty. Define it in the positive."

"I guess I can't," said Peter. "Or maybe I'm just too tired."

"Even so," said Batch. "Which idea is marked by a bug stain? I know of no idea that is bug-stained."

"There are plenty of bug-stained ideas!" stated Mercy Merry, sitting forward, impaling her pie with her fork, "And plenty that are dusty, dirty, and with smudges."

"*Which* ones?"

"The ones that are not clear," she said. "Of course."

"Yes, of course," he said. "It's all circular, isn't it? Really, we cannot speak of a clear idea without its counterpart—the unclear idea."

"My paper, then," said Mercy Merry, "lacks bug stains, smudges, dirt, or dust. Is that your opinion? Is that what you mean?"

"Basically," said Professor Batch. "I found no debris in it that stuck to the window—if I may put it that way."

Mercy Merry touched Professor Batch's hand, and patted it. "You are a good professor, sir. A very good one." She moved over to kiss him on the cheek.

He reddened. "And why is *that*?"

"It's something I wanted to say. There's no basis for it. I just felt I wanted to say it." She finished her pie in silence.

"And yet," said Professor Batch, "I feel better for your having said it. I feel . . . well, energized by it."

"Don't take it too seriously," she said, wiping her lips with a napkin.

"But I want to," he said. "However nonsensical it might be."

"It's not nonsensical."

"Oh—and why?"

"It makes sense as much as anything else makes sense."

"But doesn't anything else make sense?"

"In ways."

Professor Batch patted her shoulder as he reinserted his pipe in his mouth. He left.

"He's such a good professor," said Mercy Merry. "And so are you."

"Do you mean that?" he asked.

"Are you really writing about the Finger?"

He stood up. "Yes. More coffee?"

"Large."

"It's my life now. My professional life."

"Don't pin it down so," she said.

"What do you mean?"

"How is it *professional*? What's professional?"

"It's my *life*, then?"

"In what sense?"

"True," he said.

He went for coffee—large ones for both of them.

8

The phone rang.

Six in the morning.

"Something happened."

Sheila.

"What?"

"I was standing in front of the vanity, see. Applying my Women's Products—you know, the ones I bought at the Compendium. I often do that—stand in front of the vanity. I often study myself. Study my pores. Study my build. I'm nice to look at, aren't I? *I* think so. Anyway, I was doing this daily thing, and it suddenly dawned on me. You don't really know me. You, Peter, *knew* me. But you don't *know* me—not now. I—the *real* me, that is—am in the details. You need to live with me for at least a week or a month to watch me. Observe me. To see every little particular. I've even written them down, Peter, and maybe you could too. Like when I awaken—how do I look, with my face on the pillow? Can you tell me? And don't say *lovely*. I don't mean that."

"Write it all down? Why would someone do that?"

"*Because* how can you *really* say you know someone unless you know pretty much everything about them? I mean in the *flesh*. What is it you know? Do you know *when* I get out of bed, *how* I get out of bed, the makeup I put on first thing in the morning, what I eat for breakfast, *how* I eat it, what I drink, *when* I drink it, my hobbies, which hobby is my favorite, how I look at something—do I squint a certain way, how does my mouth look, my eyes, what are my gestures, say hands, say fingers. Just what do you know about *me*, really, Peter?"

He said he knew that she often rubbed her hands together. By now he was up and making coffee, the phone on speaker.

"Oh, good!" she said. "But why, why would I do that? What's that say about me?"

"You're worried?"

"No—not necessarily. There are different reasons to rub your hands together. What are they?"

"You're cold."

"I rubbed my hands together, *when*, the other day?"

"When you said Three Days."

"I did?"

"Yes."

"I didn't know that. That's interesting. See, there is something I don't know about myself. I'll have to write that down, Peter."

"Okay."

A silence.

"You're about as interested in me as—"

She was choking up.

"Just sleepy," he said. "I need my coffee." He tried to sound soothing.

"We don't know a thing about each other until we can describe all kinds of outward manifestations. I don't know a thing about you, Peter. Not a thing."

"A few basic facts?"

"But the observable—the body, Peter, its various gestures and movements, its stops and starts, its postures and presences—it's like reading a map."

"From the literature?" he asked.

"Yes. *Of course!*"

"Okay."

"I'll give you another extension," she said. "But we'll need to live together a while. I'll let you know when."

"What?"

The phone went dead.

9

He grew fearful. She was closing in.
Don't answer the phone.

He made a pact with himself.

He broke it.

"What you've done," she told him, "is alienation of affection."

She was in town. They were back at the bar.

"How so?" He would let this one play itself out. He would dispassionately watch where it went.

"Think about it," she said. "What does that mean?"

"I've rejected you."

"In ways."

"But not totally."

"In *important* ways. I was guilty of it too, but I made amends. Have you?"

"I tried."

"How?"

"Well, maybe I didn't."

"I assure you that you didn't. You've stomped on my feelings like they didn't matter in the least."

"But," he said, "you just said, 'in ways.' In other words, not in *all* ways."

"Funny how you remember what you *want* to remember. I'll leave it to you to remember what I *really* said."

A challenge. He rose to it. "You said in *important* ways, but what important ways?"

"You don't know?"

"You mean back then?"

"Now what do you think?"

"But that was so long ago. We must put the past behind us. The past is the past." Tautological, admittedly, but nonetheless, who could argue with it?

"And why does time make any difference?"

"It doesn't?"

She took his hand and rubbed it. "Does it really? What if you'd done something really bad back then?"

"I thought I did."

"You did. But what if it had been . . . even worse?"

"It wasn't."

"Imagine, though. If you can. If you've a mind to."

"I'd rather not."

"Let's say you'd slapped me. Would time make any difference?"

"No. But I wouldn't do such a thing." He gripped her hand. It gave him a buzz.

"But let's say you did. *Would* it make any difference? Just because it happened *back then*? And don't tell me time heals all wounds. My stupid ex said that over and over until I thought I'd *puke*."

"But in a way, doesn't it?"

"Time congeals, but only apparently—in our minds, not our hearts. Wounds fester."

"The literature?"

"*Yes. Must* you?"

"How is the mind different from the heart?"

She removed her hand and stuck her chest with a finger. The nail was bright pink. "Here's the heart. The mind can't touch it."

"Really."

"The mind knows not what the heart knows."

He didn't ask. "I hope you've forgiven me," he said.

And suddenly they were back, the two of them, sitting in the Pub. Him, her. Touching, talking, feeling.

"Let me ask again, if you'd slapped me—"

"We must take that as a given?"

"Take it any way you want. If you'd done that, wouldn't you be guilty today, this minute, sitting here with me?"

"But what if I had apologized?"

"Some things you can't apologize for."

"Like slapping?"

"That's one."

"If it were a reaction gone awry? Unpremeditated? A muscle spasm?"

"No excuse."

"Well," he said, "I didn't do that."

"It would have been kinder."

"But I thought you said—"

"Please, Peter. *Please.*"

"But you surely got over it. *Didn't you*?"

"I did not. But even if I did, the harm was *done.*"

"You went on, though, to marry. You got over me. You had another life."

"In the past tense?"

"You have a life."

"What life?"

Peter hesitated. "I don't know."

"I never forgave you. To be abandoned when you'd *known* me four thousand times or something."

"Four thousand? Or four hundred?"

"Why's the exact count make any difference? I *experienced* it as four thousand. Isn't that just as real as four hundred?"

"Not to me." He'd calculated it before: Eighteen months, at twenty times a month. He'd rounded it off to four hundred. Probably it was more like five hundred, but it *wasn't* four thousand.

"And now here you are putting a wedge between us."

"Wedge?"

"I can feel it, feel it deeply, right here." She removed her hand and grabbed his, pinioning the two together, thrusting them against her chest—hard.

He felt her ample bosom.

"Oh," he said. "Oh, I *am* sorry."

"I'm not begging. I never beg. But know your obligations."

"Obligations?"

"Yes—obligations. Think of feelings. Think of these feelings as electric circuitry in us, and when they get stomped on, it's like crimping a wire. Things don't work anymore."

"The literature?"

"Yes, yes. But why must you say it practically every minute? It's so true, isn't it? Feelings? How you can feel so bad. When you've got an overload because things are clogging up. Feelings have to be respected. Feelings are the most important thing in the world."

She stared at him—waiting for this to sink in?

"Feelings are important," he said. "I agree."

"Do you respect your students' feelings?"

"Oh, yes, I do," he said. "Certainly."

"But you don't give a flying fig about mine?"

He stared at her. A trap, of course.

"Yes, I do," he said.

"How is that?"

"I do. And I'll try to respect your feelings—from now on."

She smiled brightly. "I think I'm ready for another drink."

He ordered refills. When they came, they held hands and drank down a third, then set down their drinks.

They were back in history. In the Pub. He wanted her. But how much of it was the sexually arousing pomegranate perfume? Ah, he thought, it behooved her to keep a full supply of that on hand.

"You could do me one favor," she said.

"What is that?"

"I need my good feelings back. That man of mine—my ex—he hurt me so much. And I couldn't help but think of his abandonment as you all over again. So . . . you must promise never to abandon me again. You must promise that. *Promise.*"

He cogitated on this.

He thought of Mercy Merry.

He thought of the Assistant Dean.

"What does that mean, exactly?" he asked.

"Don't lead me on. You know what it means. I'd rather be told the truth. That would hurt, and I'd suffer the crimped circuitry for a while, perhaps a long while, but at least I wouldn't *expect* and then be let down. There is nothing worse."

"*Nothing?*" he said.

"Our feelings," she said. "That's all we have—really have. *Thinginess.* Don't you get it? It's in our very blood. Our sensory receivers. I want to *feel, feel, feel*: me, me, me. I want to know I'm alive, Peter!"

"Sure," he said. "Sure."

"We won't be alive forever."

"I know."

That was where they left it.

10

Perhaps now wasn't the time to develop something with the Assistant Dean. But he longed for the scent of her hair, the soft touch of her lips.

And so he invited Lucinda Marigold to come over to his apartment for the upcoming Friday.

"Oh, certainly," she said. "Yes. I'll be there. When?"

"At six. If that's good."

"Good. I will cook for you."

He hadn't expected this. It was but a mere whim. A fantasy.

He tidied up the place, vacuumed the carpets, washed the windows, stocked up wine. He cleaned the bathroom, made the bed carefully.

Would she . . . the Assistant Dean?

It seemed improbable.

And now, he thought, what you must do is put aside these preparations and get back to your project: the Finger.

But the Assistant Dean, the Assistant Dean:

You must not tell the Assistant Dean about the Finger.

Axiomatic.

But what about the meeting with the Dean? The Dean had written him about an update. The time for that update was fast approaching.

That progress report:

Be vague with the Dean.

The Finger is too crude to mention to the Dean.

But wouldn't this mean circumlocution?

Or couldn't this mean circumvention?

Hems, haws, guttural, gravelly whispering?

Questionable behavior in the Dean's office?

How low could you whisper?

What if the Dean urged louder whispering?

What if the Dean shouted out the whispered words?

You could close the door.

But could you close the door? Its being the Dean's office, not yours?

You could certainly ask that the door be closed.

Of course you could.

Ah, problem solved.

He went on to his project. It was difficult to get the Assistant Dean's odiferous hair out of his mind. Maybe it was a good thing, that odor. It charged him up. He wrote better. He wrote faster.

Perhaps the Assistant Dean won't care if you mention the Finger, its being an icon?

What business does the Assistant Dean have in your project anyway?

How is the Finger her business?

Good. Problem solved.

He wrote away.

Finally, a publication.

There is no question that inspiration is the first requirement for starting.

There is no question that the second requirement, good work, is also contingent on inspiration.

Work that lacks it is stale work.

He looked forward to Friday. He wrote way into the night.

He feared reading over the pages.

He felt a sense of having pierced the veil. The icon, in all its mystery, was made more real, given more depth. Its symbolism was made rich.

Manifold.

The Finger was posing new questions.

Birds flew into it. Bird feathers stuck to it. Birds pooped on it.

It was wrapped with kite string and kites beating against its concrete tower.

A sky divers club of fifty jumpers were planning to do a ring around it.

He worked at the conundrums.

11

He was to appear at Grocery Kingdom. The Assistant Dean wrote him an email that read:

> Good morning, Professor Boatz:
> You will recall that Grocery Kingdom is interested in a corporate liaison with your department. Please meet with Mr. Wexler, Marketing Manager, at 9 a.m., Friday, to discuss this matter. If this doesn't fit with your schedule, please contact me in a timely manner.
> Cordially,
> Lucinda Marigold, Ph.D.
> Assistant Dean

How formal and stiff for a woman who would soon—a few days hence—be fixing him supper. But, he reasoned, perhaps the Assistant Dean's emails were under scrutiny—perhaps by the Dean himself. He forgave her.

Grocery Kingdom offices had a college campus appearance, a huge green manicured lawn of several acres, the office building itself three stories high of glass and steel, with the Grocery Kingdom logo (in a cursive scrawl) and the familiar slogan: *Our Kingdom Includes You!*

Peter walked up the wide sidewalk, with not one visible crack, toward the mighty arched entrance.

Mr. Wexler was a tiny man with a weasel face. He constantly wiped his nose with a handkerchief, which he kept stuffed in one hand.

They had coffee in his spacious office, decorated with framed pictures of various food items: a loaf of sliced bread, banana, orange, cucumber, hot dog, ice cream bar—and several others, but Mr. Wexler interrupted him before he could see the others.

"Professor Boatz, I cannot express my enthusiasm enough.

It's so pleasing to see the university make contact with business. I have several university professor liaisons, but when the President mentioned icons, I thought, 'Icons. Why, of course. Isn't everything we do here marketing-wise at GK a matter of icons?' Sliced bread, packaged meat, frozen vegetables, ice cream in the container, toilet paper on the roll—we forget how iconic each is. How they each speak for a generation of consumers! Marvelous, isn't it? Now, could you tell me about your own icons of choice? Your present interest, perhaps?"

"Icons of power," said Peter.

"Oh? As in?"

"A cruise missile, for instance."

"Cruise missile?" Mr. Wexler wiped his nose. "No, I doubt that would be of use." He smiled brightly. "But I do like the images of power idea. I like that very much. Could you give me other examples?"

"Nuclear bomb."

"Well, no."

"Uzi."

"Ah, ah—well." Mr. Wexler scribbled on his legal pad. "You know, we do have surveillance equipment at all of our retail outlets to record the movements of armed men—and we do not rule out the appearance of such extreme weaponry as this."

"Brass knuckles."

"Oh, heavens no. But do you not have anything more pleasant? Something more . . . food-oriented?"

None of the food groups called to Peter's mind an icon of power. But then he had it: "Gated mansion? Grocery *Kingdom*?"

"Gated—?"

"*Kingdom*."

Mr. Wexler prodded his lips with his finger. "My, my. The gate to the Kingdom?"

"Yes, exactly." Peter sipped his coffee.

"What a splendid idea. Customers would certainly feel special. Once they got past that gate."

"With a customer password."

Mr. Wexler grew serious. "The cost would be prohibitive, I'm afraid. And what if you forgot your password?"

"You don't eat. *Or* you go to another store."

"Oh—heavens no. We couldn't have that. Absolutely not."

Peter shrugged.

"Icons of power. Is that all you have to offer?"

"It's where my mind is presently."

Mr. Wexler gave it some thought. He wiped his mouth. "Food," he said, "*is* power. Isn't it?"

Peter's eyes drifted to a picture he hadn't seen before. A tomato. He stood up and pointed a finger at it. "You can throw that," he said. "At detested individuals and parties."

"Oh, please, no," said Mr. Wexler.

"I mean the tomato."

"Oh!"

"It's food—and it's an icon."

"How so?"

"A rotten tomato?"

"Oh, but we don't wish to suggest such a thing!" said Mr. Wexler. "And really, unless you have something more positive—"

"Rotten tomatoes redress things that need redressing," said Peter. "And they're less potent than cannonballs."

"I see your point."

"Or cruise missiles."

Mr. Wexler nodded.

"They could be used in advertising. Food isn't only to be eaten—"

"Well—still, Professor—"

"*Know your uses of food. One is power.* How's that for a slogan?"

"Thank you for your time," said Mr. Wexler.

Peter's eye caught the banana cream pie picture in a dessert foursome.

"Almost any food can be used for power," said Peter. "Cream pies, most famously."

"I think that concludes our meeting," said Mr. Wexler.

"When we think cream pie, what's the first thing that comes to mind? Seriously?" He pointed at the foursome.

"Oh, I know, I *know*," said Mr. Wexler, turning his head. "But I do wish it wasn't that way."

"But it is," said Peter. "Cream pies are truly iconic."

12

The knock came with a deliberateness that at first surprised him. It made him wonder if it was the police, a collector, the apartment manager, or some sort of authority. But it was only *her*—Lucinda Marigold. She was to come, he'd been expecting her, but he certainly hadn't expected three hard knocks like that.

"I've got some things," she said, hefting a sack. "I'll just take them to your kitchen." She headed straight that way. It was a small kitchen and visible from the door, so you could not exactly miss it.

He watched her drop the things on the kitchen counter and then gather up some of it, open the refrigerator, and stick them in just as though she lived there.

She exited the kitchen.

She noticed his desk piled high with books and composition books.

"Oh, you've been writing," she said. "Are you progressing?"

"Some."

"It's going to be heavily academic, I take it."

"Of course."

"*Well.* I really don't think I'd do an *academic* study—aren't academic studies generally pretty dry?"

Odd, he thought, coming from a dean—or rather, assistant dean. And hadn't she been all for it when he'd encountered her in the Faculty Club? "They don't *have* to be, do they?"

"If you can capture the essence, the universal, the real thing— no. But *can* you?"

"I hope to."

"Good for you. I tried, but I couldn't. I gave up and turned to fiction. Then memoir. It was wonderful. Marvelous. I captured the essence—not the particulars: the essence. Now I'm writing poetry. I'm capturing the essence there too. That's what you must do: capture the essence—if you can."

What a blitz.

"So you've published—"

"Nothing. They don't want the essence. I ought to know— after being turned down for five books! They want the particulars. But you must go for the essence anyway."

"Yes," he said. "We do have to be faithful to our vision."

"You think so?"

"How about some wine?"

"I brought some. Red. White too. Please fix us both a glass. That would be so kind."

"Of course." He hurried to the kitchen. He got the cork out.

He came back with full glasses. He handed her one.

"Thank you. You have a nice view."

"I know."

"You do think so?"

"Yes, I do."

"The street. Two nice big oaks there. Oh, look, there's a cat."

"Lives down there. Right below me."

"They allow pets here?"

"No."

"Oh, my. Then the cat's not long for this world, is it?"

"Haven't caught him yet."

"Since when?"

"Three years. At least."

"How long have you lived here?"

"Five . . . I don't know, maybe six years. No, seven. It's seven."

"My, my. Sit down."

He was still standing, with her sitting staring up at him.

"Oh, yes." He sat down across from her, and then planted his shoes on the floor.

"If I drink this, I'll be out," she said.

"Oh, but what about eating?"

"Oh, yes, and I *am* hungry. I promised pasta. I'll do that. I'll go in there, in a minute, and I'll do it. But first, just this glass of wine. Do you ever wonder why people eat, eat, eat, drink, drink, drink? Isn't that odd? Just like animals, we are."

"Yes. I've found it rather odd. The continual cycle of it. Over and over, day to day, week to week, month to month, year to year, decade to decade. Millennia to millennia. But I guess we *are* animals."

"Of course. But eat, eat, eat. I'm always hungry. Aren't you?"

"Most of the time."

"I'm always thirsty. I can't help but drink one thing after another—whatever the law will permit. It seems so silly—really, if you think about it. Why can't we be self-sustaining?"

"I wonder the same thing."

"Coffee?" she said.

"I can't do without it."

"I want . . . do you know what I want?"

"What?"

"Something intensely good. At some point I'd like something intensely good. As far as eating and drinking. But then you don't find a thing that is intensely good, do you? It's always up here," she said, tapping her forehead. "You know it, but you can't find it. It's all a letdown. Pasta, for instance. But I couldn't think of anything else. You think *pasta*—you envision it—but the real pasta is never as good as the ideal pasta—the one you see in your head. The ideal pasta has a kind of transcendental quality to it unsurpassed by any pasta ever made. Don't you agree?"

"But it *is* good. Usually, I mean."

"Up to a point. But I've been tiring of just *good* lately. I've been wanting more, as I said. I've been wanting perfect. I'm stuck in the perfect. You can't satisfy me. Try as you might. Silly, isn't it?"

"Well."

"I'm not easy to get along with. Sorry, but it's true."

They stared out the window onto the sidewalk below.

"That cat is still out there. I hope he doesn't get hit. Smashed. Obliterated."

"He's survived all these years."

"Three, I think you said."

"That's right."

"I'd better get up and get in there and make the damn pasta."

He dashed off the wine. He refilled. She eyed him, then smiled—but just slightly.

He exited the kitchen.

She was fixing the pasta. From the living room, he saw her elbows going. He saw her neck the way it was now and then exposed when her hair swung from side to side. He judged her hands to be firm and grasping. He imagined her strong and aggressive, and yet he also imagined her as suddenly, in a fit of emotion, cracking. He swept the image out of his head.

13

She was coming all the time now. She would arrive about five, leave her car parked on the street below, and he'd hear her steps on the stairs. Then the measured steps down the hall and three hard knocks on the door. He opened the door. She came in, dropped her purse on the chair. Sat down, removed her shoes.

She would then say, "I could sure use something to drink."

"What would you want?"

"Wine?"

"I've got some." Because he kept it stocked now.

"I hope it's cold."

It was a ritual. "Yes," he said. He kept plenty of it cold.

He brought her a glass of white wine. She thanked him. Stood up, moved toward the window. She always sat at the window before fixing supper.

"How is the work coming?" she would ask.

And he told her. "It's coming along."

"How far did you get today?" She leaned a little out the window. "Where is the cat?"

"I don't know. I haven't seen him."

"How far? How many pages?"

"Oh, several. I wrote four or five hours."

"Well, that's good. Very good. Will you ever show me what you wrote? I'd be interested, you know."

"Sure. Once I'm finished."

"I think it will be good. Very good. As long as it's passionate with ideas, as long as it's the Grand Narrative. There I said it. I believe firmly in the Grand Narrative, in the totalizing account. Don't you?"

"Yes," he said. "But I feel condemned by it. I feel as though I've missed the mark somehow."

"How so?" She took a gulp of wine.

"What have I done? What have I ever done but explicate a

vision? And what if that vision calls for duty of some sort? What duty have I performed? What duties neglected?"

"The objective yardstick. Measured with fine precision."

"Yes."

"But isn't that enough?"

"What?"

"To articulate it?"

"Maybe not. Maybe I need to commit—to take charge, however unlike me this would be."

"Oh, cut the melodrama. Write the book. That's commitment enough."

He refilled his wine glass. It was the wine speaking, of course. He tended to grandstand when he was buzzed.

"You want action?" she said. "Jam it down their throats. Jam your vision down their throats!" Her words were beginning to slur.

"Jam?"

"Down their throats!"

He spoke of eating.

"You know what we have to do, don't you?" she asked.

"What?"

"Tear it all down. Every bit of it. Start over."

"Tear what down?"

"Everything. It all needs to come down!"

He loved the finality about the woman. He told her about the Finger. It gushed out of him. A sublime monstrosity, he cried.

She stared at him. "Yes—I've read about it. Well, I guess it's a start. Iconic? Yes, perhaps, though hardly decent and bolstering to the human spirit. In fact, degrading, isn't it? But I can understand a professor of icons taking some interest in it."

Why had he gushed?

"Naturally," he said, and smiled.

"I must say that I doubt, at the practical level, it will make an ounce worth of difference. Do you?"

"I can't say. Has anything ever?"

"And you mean by that?"

"In history. It's always the same, isn't it? Always at issue?"

"And so?"

"Rage," he said. "Its manifestation. It's an icon of power. One among many."

"I guess that partakes of the eternal."

"More Fingers are rising," he pointed out. "Finger Two, Finger Three, and so on."

"The more the merrier?"

They sat down to eat.

When she left, he listened for her feet in the hall, then on the stairs.

14

News article: "Today, the Finger Jump Skydivers jumped five thousand feet circling the Finger. Hands were held, necklace-like, until they came to a bump on the ground. One male jumper, age twenty-five, exclaimed: 'This was it! We did it! The Finger lives on!' Another jumper, a female, age twenty-eight, proclaimed: 'This is a historic event. If you're a rich pig watching this, you think twice. You just think twice!'"

News item: "The Second Finger Jump will occur on Saturday, Aug. 1. It's expected to draw a crowd of ten thousand people. The organizer of the Jump, Bayford Bailey, stated: 'On this second historic jump, we're going to come down humming *OM*. It'll bring tears to your eyes. You bet it will. We've done it before. People cry. They actually cry. You watch and see if they don't.'"

News item: "Mr. Finger stated today that he will send sprayers up the Finger to reduce the bird excrement. Said Mr. Finger, 'How this bird excrement builds up I really have no idea. Somehow birds of all kinds seem drawn to pooping on my monument. It's a letdown. Really, why does nature itself seem to be against us? Is it really in nature to advance those who have and take away from those who do not?' Asked if this monument didn't itself represent a vast expenditure of funds, Mr. Finger stated: 'This money comes from millions of folks who chipped in as little as one dollar to see this event—and I do consider it an event—take place. These folks gave what they could.'"

Peter wondered:

Here I am writing when I could be at the Finger. Here I am crafting words, when I could be humming OM. Here I am age thirty-five, and I need to make a decision. And what would that be? I am what I am. And I'm happy with it. Only I want to hum OM. Will this be the only time?

But what if you cried? Would crying be okay?

"Yes, it would be *okay*," said Sheila the next time she met him at the bar. "What's wrong with a man crying?"

"Nothing."

"My ex never cried. Not once. That might be the reason we didn't stay together. I like men who cry—just now and then. Not constantly. I don't mean constantly turning on the faucet. I think that's disgusting."

"But cry at what?"

"Well, not at *OM*," she said. "You cry at that, something's wrong with you. I mean you're disturbed or something."

"Oh, I don't know," he said.

"Bob—he's into crap like that."

"He is?"

"I don't know why. Midlife crisis, I guess. And Lee, that poor woman. He's so unfaithful."

"He is?"

"Sixteen or seventeen, something like that, affairs. I don't know why she stays with him. I wouldn't put up with that for a minute!"

"No, no," he said.

"You'd never do that, would you?"

"No."

"Bob's not a bad guy, though, I don't mean that. I like him. In fact, I love the guy. You can't help but love the guy."

"Um."

"He's so . . . nice. And I'm not afraid to say that he's pretty . . . well, manly. Don't you think so, you being a man?"

"Well, I don't know about that."

"What don't you know?"

"I'm not exactly a judge on what's manly, what's not."

"Hmm, I'd think that most men would be. I mean really, what's it come down to? Isn't it what's not *feminine*? You have your testosterone, your muscles, your deeper voice. That's for starters. And Bob, he's got the muscles—you saw that when you went swimming with him. Didn't you?"

"I didn't pay that much attention."

"Oh, come on. Of *course* you did. He's built like a . . . I don't know what." She leaned over and whispered. "Lee's told me things. Pretty . . . well . . . pretty—" She laughed. "But I can't exactly repeat them."

"Don't then."

"Use your imagination."

"I'd rather not."

"Okay, where were we? What's manly—you were asking."

"You were telling."

"Oh—well, besides the big three, which I just mentioned, there is a fourth." She fingered his chest with a speculative probe.

"Yes?"

"It's treating a woman the way she wishes to be treated. And knowing, damn it, without having to be told. A real man always *knows*. A real man never *asks*. *Never.*"

"Like what?"

"Like what? I have to tell you this?"

"I'd appreciate it if you would."

"Okay—certain come-ons. Animal behaviors. The animals, they *know*. What happened to male homo sapiens that they have to ask?"

"Ask what?"

"Oh, come on."

"What?"

"Like," she whispered. "Do you *want* it?"

"Hmm."

"He *knows* she wants it. He doesn't have to go and *ask*. God! I hate it when men do that!"

"Uh," he said, "men?"

"Oh, sorry—my ex. For fifteen years, he'd come around and say, 'Hey, babe, want it?' What say?' You don't think I got tired of *that*?"

"But Bob—"

"Bob would know. Bob does know."

"He does?"

"He goes after what he wants—and he doesn't waste time either. My ex?"

"Yes?"

"He'd say that, and then pretty soon I'm upstairs in the bedroom waiting, naked, under the covers. But he's not there. What's that prick doing?"

"I don't know. What?"

"Exactly. And when I press it, calling down, he's yelling, 'Up in a minute. Just a minute, damn it!' And he was the one who'd asked for it in the first place!"

"Not good," said Peter.

"But Bob, he's a man enough, he doesn't waste any time."

"Oh," said Peter.

She flushed. "Look, don't get any ideas. Okay? I'm talking hypothetically."

Her finger kept working at his chest.

"We could go out to my motel," she said.

"We could?"

"Damn!" she said, retracting her finger. "You know what Bob would have said? If I had said that very thing?"

"What?"

"Nothing. He would have risen, paid the bill, patted me one, and we'd left together. There would be no point in saying anything? Other than, 'Where's your motel, honey?' And maybe patting my knee on the way out."

"I let you down, then?" said Peter.

"You've changed," said Shelia. "What the hell happened? I don't get it."

"What?"

"I just don't get it."

15

"We're having a little party," said Mercy Merry.

"Oh?"

"At my house. Are you coming? It's Friday."

But on Friday Lucinda Marigold wanted him to read portions of his manuscript, and then afterwards *pore over it at her favorite bar*. "I want to see just what you're up to," she had said. "A kind of interim report." The Assistant Dean in her was coming out.

"I can't on Friday," he said.

"How about Saturday?" said Mercy Merry.

"But isn't the party Friday?"

"It doesn't have to be. I want you there."

On Saturday the Assistant Dean was spending the whole day at a conference a hundred miles off.

He hesitated. But then he said, "I guess I could."

"Good. Real nice. Then it'll be Saturday."

"What's my role exactly?"

"Why you're so special?"

"Yes."

"I want a corrective. I want a heavy. I want someone, please, to stomp on that one simpleton in case she ups and shoots her mouth off."

"Joyce Early?"

"Yes. She's driving me nuts with the ever-so-clear but uninvestigated Grand Narrative she spouts."

"Spouts?"

"Assumes—anyway."

"I'm a firm believer in the Grand Narrative myself."

"But you've been tested. You've been tried and tested, and you've emerged, fully feathered, with this. This is *you*. You know the literature."

"She's learning the literature."

They were in the Faculty Club having coffee. Mercy Merry had become a regular coffee drinking member of the Club, refusing to pay idle respect to silly rules.

"Show me any evidence of that."

"You don't think so?"

"You have to read tons and tons of literature, and then you don't parrot back what you read. You rip and snort at it. Does she rip and snort?"

"No?"

"Reading the literature is attacking the literature."

"I see what you mean. But do I attack?"

"You cannot know without attacking. You know so you've attacked."

"Flawless logic."

She took his hand. "You are my favorite professor."

He wiggled free. "Really," he said.

"Oh, don't be so bound by stupid conventions!"

"Attack them?"

"Yes, please."

She kissed him quickly and departed.

16

Time now to meet with the Dean. "An update," the Dean had said, "just an update. An interim. Nothing to fret about."

Dean Chasm leaned forward at his desk with his hands spread forth. His hands looked like nervous birds about to take flight.

"The project," he said, "the book. It's quite important to get this project, this book, off the ground this summer, and so I'm wanting to know, how is it going? *Is* it going? *Is* something good happening? Is *anything* really happening?"

"Uh, yes," said Peter. He did have thirty or so pages. He hoped to have fifty a few days hence, in time for the Assistant Dean's perusal—making the bar postmortem a more delightful experience. Fifty good pages, he thought, fifty good ones.

"Deadlines," said the Dean.

He nodded. "Fifty good pages. It's underway and sailing just fine."

"And could you, if you don't mind my asking," said the Dean, doing spider hops with his fingers, "tell me more about this book. See, the Committee will ask. Of course, they'll ask. They like the concrete, you see, always the concrete. You can appreciate that, can't you? Coffee, by the way?"

"Uh, yes."

"I'm sorry I didn't ask before. Here," and he grabbed up a cup and set it down on the desktop, rather hard, Peter thought. The man seemed to be greatly on edge today.

Peter noticed the door was open, and he could see the Assistant Dean's hand clutching a cup—was it hot tea? The cup disappeared, and then it was set back down. It disappeared. And then again, it was set back down.

"Have some coffee, have some hot brew," shouted the Dean. "Here, I'll have a cup right along with you!"

They stood together at the pot, and the Dean placed a hand on his shoulder. "You're a valuable member of the faculty, sir. Dr. Marigold speaks highly of you."

"Good," said Peter.

"Have a seat," he said, once they both had their cups filled to the brim.

Peter sat and sipped. He saw the Assistant Dean's door close.

"Now, when, when, *when*, is this thing going to sprout, flower, and seed?" asked the Dean.

"Fifty good pages," said Peter. "And advancing."

"Good, good, very good. And what's it about? What's it all about? Specifically, that is. Icons, didn't you say—"

"Icons of power."

"Oh, yes, my notes here . . . someplace. Tell me again. Icons of power. Specifics. Specifics, please. The world turns on specifics."

"Yes," said Peter. "Admittedly."

"Good." The Dean leaned back with his hands behind his head. "You know, Professor Boatz, it's a good world. A very good world. Isn't it?"

"Yes. A good one."

"You can do a lot of stuff in a world like this. Don't you agree?"

"Yes—you can."

"I can see right now: cities, towns, plains, mountains, rivers, woods—the manufactured as well as the natural environment. I can feel it all beckoning. Don't you?"

The Dean's eyes were fixed on something on the wall. Peter turned and looked. What was it?

"Try and do. Try and do. That's how the job is done, Professor. Uh, Professor Boatz. That's how the job is and has *always* been done. Try and do."

"I agree."

"And so . . . what specifics? Give me tangibles. Something I can take to the hungry Committee."

"Well," said Peter. "Let me think: the castle, the hunt, the torture chamber, the Virgin, the cross—"

"Torture chamber?"

"Iconic."

"How? Oh, sorry, it's your area. Sorry, Professor. You'd know about these things, not me. But how? What else?"

"The Finger," said Peter.

"Pardon?"

"Mr. Finger building the Finger," said Peter. "Have you heard?"

"You're using that?"

"Iconic."

"Ah, ah—well, but it's so . . . common. So coarse. And yet—yes, we sometimes do begin with the common, the coarse. That is all we have. We must after all begin somewhere. And so . . . with you it's this Finger."

"Yes, but I will end there as well."

"End there?"

"Yes."

"Well, but . . . well, I expect the Committee will be pleased. To have something. Instead of nothing. And putting the nature of that something squarely in your court. You being the professor, as it were. But, odd, though."

"What's that?"

"Odd why anyone would do that. Such huge capital investment." The Dean's liquid blue eyes fastened on him. Peter imagined diving into them.

"Donations," said Peter. "One to ten dollars."

"Yes, yes," said the Dean, "but still—"

They sat and sipped their coffee.

Peter saw that the Dean was now looking out the window. In the distance there was a water tower. The Dean pointed. "Higher than that, so much higher than that. Just consider. Will you provide photos?"

"Maybe."

"It's a vision, isn't it?" said the Dean. "Someone had a vision." He swiveled around quickly. "Someone had a vision and said, 'Do it! Do it!' That's what it takes. You do it or you don't!" He stood up and extended a hand.

Peter took it, and shook it. He thought his hand would break.

"Do it!" said the Dean. "Launch that book. This summer, now. Don't tarry."

"No," said Peter.

"Vision. We grab what we want. We don't ask questions. Do we?"

"No—we don't."

"Let me show you something." He placed a fatherly hand on Peter's shoulder. "Here, here somewhere."

The Dean took a book down. It had a purple cover. He opened it and gingerly paged through it. "Here's a chapter. 'Happiness Knocks. Are You Ready?'"

"Sure," said Peter.

"My chapter—the title," said the Dean.

"Oh—yes," said Peter.

"Yes, yes. There's vision here, Professor. Ample vision. We hear the knock. Do we answer? If you have ears to hear, we do. Otherwise, we don't. But that's only one thought. It's all about *chemistry*. Ever study chemistry?"

"Yes."

"Chemistry has to do with acids, bases, reagents—that sort of thing. The world's one big chemical stew, Professor. As are we ourselves. Humans are one big chemical stew. What's important is getting the right chemical mix. You mix A and B, you get a happy man. You mix A and C, you get an unhappy man. Know your chemicals."

"So it's *all* chemicals?"

"I didn't say that. Some things we don't want to be happy about." He tapped his head. "Choose your chemicals. Choose them carefully." He led Peter to the window.

"That tower," said the Dean.

"Yes."

"A man with the wrong chemicals wouldn't see what I see."

"What do you see?"

"Power. Strength. The will to achieve. That's what I see."

"And the man with the wrong chemicals?"

"A water tower. Plain and simple. Nothing to discuss. Nothing to feel angst over."

"Angst?"

"There's always angst. Isn't there?"

"Yes."

"Which university press?"

"Pardon?"

"For your book?"

"Uh, none right now."

"Get a press. Get one lined up, Professor. Unpublished manuscripts don't get the job done. *Publication*. Of course you know that. Of course I'm not telling you something you don't know."

"Of course."

"I'll let the Committee know."

They shook hands. Peter got his hand loose.

When he made his way out, the Assistant Dean's office door was still closed.

17

Mercy Merry could certainly throw a decent party, Peter thought. She had the small white frame house stocked with booze, and wall to wall with people, over fifty of them. The talk ran to: Classes— bad ones, confusing ones, easy ones, grossly difficult ones. Loves— aspired to, in limbo, in doubt, in wreckage, long since buried. Drinks—bad ones, ones you could do without, ones you couldn't. Houses—big ones, little ones like this one, ones hit by storms, ones rotting down, ones recently erected, ones residents recently evicted from.

He clutched drinks, pontificated, listened in, interrupted, was revered, was reviled. He stayed afterwards when Mercy Merry whispered in his ear, with a wet tongue. "You could, you know, *linger?*"

He had never thought of her in this way. That is, as a possible. And now he could only think of her in this way.

She took him into her dark bedroom. The moon shone on the hills that descended below the house. They lay down on the bed.

"Now," she said. "Now, you shall become more than my professor."

A trap, he thought. A trap, surely.

"I need a drink," he said.

"A drink? After all that?"

"One more."

"Nervous, are you?"

"Just one drink," he said.

"Why of course," she said. "A drink. Why of course."

A woman with a plan, he thought.

They had a few.

They had a few more.

She guided him back to her bed. The moon had risen. The bed was pooled with light.

He had real hopes now, he said. But not just hopes. A big

book. A reality. A hot item. "You'll see me in the Icon Hall of Fame," he rhapsodized.

He'd gotten a real buzz.

"Is there such a thing?"

"No, but maybe there ought to be."

"That's nice," she said. "A big professor. With a big book."

"Big," he said.

"About that Finger," she said.

"Yes."

"You've never even seen it. Have you?"

"No."

"Don't you think," she said, "you ought to at least *see* it?"

"Sure."

"When?"

"Sometime."

"You'd rather not see it," she said.

"No. I do want to see it."

"Well, then?"

"What's the point, really, of seeing it?"

"That's right. All it is, is concrete and steel. That's it. Concrete and steel, regardless of any iconic meaning you've invested in it. It's just that—concrete and steel. Nothing more."

In the light of the yellow moon, he could see her luminous eyes.

"That's it, huh?"

"Not even that. What's concrete? What's steel?"

"God," he said.

"Go and look."

He couldn't help himself. She drew him like a magnet. He was filings. But then he rose quickly.

"I mustn't," he said.

"Mustn't what?"

"Got to go."

"Where?"

Back to his lonely apartment? The Assistant Dean was gone. Could he? Should he? She had leapt at his book portions—*sublime*, she had said. *You will top the charts*, she had said. But was that the liquor speaking?   Perhaps he owed her. But still, she *was* gone, and he was needy. In fact, he was desperate.

"Nowhere," he said.

"Be my professor," she said.

18

"This is the house I picked out," said Sheila.

It was a big one.

She was in town once more, and she said it was important to lay down some clear objectives. It started with where you lived. Because that was one of the Big Things, as the *Compendium* put it. The Big Things could be divided according to Tangibles and Intangibles. Tangibles were House, Utilities, Furnishings, Food, Car, Boat, and Camper. Intangibles were Salary and Savings. Electronic Beeps, these latter two, beeps in cyberspace. Ever so essential, of course, for providing the Tangibles. But don't get too caught up in Beeps. Not in Beeps themselves. "They are instrumental only."

"The *Compendium*," he said.

She ignored him.

"So," she said, "we have this house before us. Tangibles, Peter. All kinds of Tangibles. I find pretty exciting!"

"Where's the agent?"

"Gone—for a few hours. By my request. I told her *privacy*. We need *privacy*."

They looked about.

"See, right out there, I plan to build a nice deck. And a gazebo . . . out a bit farther."

He looked.

"Um," he said.

"Can't you see us out there?" she said, drawing him close.

The perfume was stronger this morning than before. He drifted toward her as she moved about.

"Now, then. I see the kitchen as the work center of this house. I want a double door refrigerator here, and pots and pans hanging here, all brass, to match the stove." She drew him to an alcove and stopped. "We'll stock the refrigerator with meat—yes, meat. Beef, Peter. Beef, beef, beef, regardless of your particular hang-ups over it. I myself don't see a problem. A man, Peter, needs his meat." She leaned toward him and gave him a long kiss. And then withdrew.

She took him to the remaining rooms on the ground floor, pointing out what she'd do with the living room, the exercise room, the small study, the two bathrooms. She handed him a slip of paper. "I've figured the cost of furnishings, all told, kitchen and these other rooms, at about thirty-five. That's a happy medium. It's not deficient and it's not excessive. But go ahead, if you think you can find a better deal."

He saw the prices and the places.

"Let's go upstairs," she whispered.

Upstairs, she led him down the hall, from bedroom to bedroom—four in all.

"Here," she said, pointing to the largest bedroom, painted in pink, "is where it all happens. This they call the Wheelhouse. This is where the production starts. And believe me, honey, it *will* start on Day One. There'll be no letup, either, once it starts. Around the clock, honey dearest, like you can't even imagine. With one object in mind. And what is that?"

"Thinginess?"

She leaned toward him, and the perfume seeped from her pores. He tried to back off but couldn't.

"No let up," she said. "None at all."

"But," he said.

"No buts."

She pulled him out of the room, and they ambled down the hall, arm in arm. "The bigger study is right there," she said. "Where all your books and highfaluting ideas can circulate around, but believe me I'll never know since you'll keep the door closed, please." She waltzed him down a few more doors.

"Now this is *my* room—and I'm not to be bothered here, just as you're not to be bothered in your special space. This will be for sewing, etcetera. For making things for the house, etcetera."

They made their way down the stairs.

"Isn't it perfectly wonderful! Isn't it?"

"Perfectly," he said.

"I can tell," she said.

"What?"

"You aren't impressed. I can see. But that's okay. Give yourself time, and you will be." She produced a second slip of paper. "Here, here's what the furnishings would be for the second floor—it's not on the cheap, but it's not like we're pretending to be rich, either."

He studied it. "Thirty-five thousand."

"That's right. Nothing's for free, you know."

She grabbed him and kissed him hard.

He was about to say, he was about to . . . but didn't. He said he had to get off right now, to get some work done on his book.

"About that awful Finger? You'd rather do that than be with me?"

He said he had to. The Dean was on him. Pressing hard.

"Dean," she said. "What's he know?"

"The Dean's on my case," said Peter.

She moved off. "You know what? You know what Bob said?"

"What?"

"He said a man who chose that Finger over me was just stupid. I hate to say that, carrying gossip, but that's what Bob said. And Bob says what he means. He doesn't fool around."

"Stupid?"

"Well, yes, because what's that Finger going to get you? You think about it. Where's that leading? Who's going to take you seriously? A professor writing about a Finger like that!"

He stared at her. "The Dean okayed it."

"Oh, that Dean."

"It will be a big book—a hot one," said Peter.

"It won't get published. No one wants a book that's so . . . disgusting."

"The discussion isn't disgusting."

"Get your mind out of the sewer."

"I don't think of it that way," he said.

"And how do you think of it?"

A car pulled up outside. A lady stepped out.

"Agent, I'll bet," he said.

"Damn it! I told her to leave us alone!"

When he was about to leave, Sheila moved in close. "You could come to my motel room," she whispered.

19

News item: "Finger One is heavily under construction. Mr. Finger expects it to reach its half mile height in a week or less."

News item: "Finger Two is over a half mile high. Finger Three is planned for a full mile. Asked whether these monoliths are safe, Mr. Finger commented: 'They're built with the highest regard for safety. And if they do fall, they'll land on our own property, on retired farm land.'"

News item: "Mr. Finger plans the biggest demonstrations yet against nuisance suits aimed at the Finger. The demonstrations will run for a full week. 'We expect thousands to turn out. Once the people are heard, Rich Man's nuisance suits are over.'"

20

"You're going where?" said Lucinda Marigold.

"To the Finger." To a big demonstration, he told her, planned to top off all previous ones—against a nuisance suit.

"That's a long way."

"Five hundred miles."

"Perhaps you'll see Mr. Finger himself."

"Gone," said Peter. "A travelling man. It's run by a crew now."

"Things in the saddle," she said. "And what about your class?"

"Dismissed for a week."

"I must issue a warning," she said. "Don't get caught up in this thing, Peter. Don't lose sight of its larger meaning. It's easy to lose sight of the higher calling when you are caught up in the passions of the particular. And there will be a lot of that. Won't there?"

He drove out, over the plains, over foothills, through mountain tunnels. He made it in one long day, arriving in the black of night against blinding motel lights. The next morning when he headed out to his car, he saw the Finger ringed by wisps of white cloud against a bluish sky.

The roads were packed with traffic. It took him three hours of slow-moving vehicles—cars, trucks, campers—to arrive at the Finger and get parked in a huge dirt lot. He got out and stood to look. Up this close he had to lean way back to see up to the Finger's top—or was that the top?—shielding his eyes from the harsh sun. This, he thought, this towering Babel of steel and concrete, was on the order of a religious experience. The shape of the tower was distinctly finger-like, with its general curvature and undulations, and he caught sight of the inside knuckle with its notable wrinkle edged in concrete. The Finger was distinctly male.

The crowd was inching toward the base of the Finger. He pushed his way through. Over the heads of the throng, he could see three simulated fingers descending and a thumb bent over, pressed against the simulated ring finger.

He was lusting to stand before the whole thing—see it all, up close.

He pushed forward against backs of humans, mobbed up. Noting how tall and brawny he was, some gave him leeway. Being a former jock, he thought, does have its upsides. A man fiftyish with his glasses sliding off his nose clutched Peter's arm: "The cops will be here any minute now. Let the crowd get big, see—you know? And then they show up in riot gear and all. Cracked a bunch of heads yesterday. Probably will today too. You ready?"

"No."

"Look at that jam coming."

More and more cars arriving, parking, people getting out.

"Probably half of them's here just for the spectacle of it. That your reason?"

"I'm just checking," said Peter.

"Checking? Checking what?"

"Checking. That's all."

"Reporter?" The man readjusted his glasses. Then he went for Peter's elbow.

"No—professor."

"Professor. Of what? The Finger? Ha! Ha!"

Strained chuckle.

The man tightened his grip on Peter's elbow. Peter could feel fear oozing from the man's fingers.

Sirens were wailing now.

"There you go. What'd I tell you?"

A man was working his way through the crowd with a box. He'd hand something to someone, collect dollar bills, and then move on to the next.

"Selling miniatures," said the man. "Cash only, no cards."

"Miniature—"

"Fingers. Souvenirs. You know. They got tee-shirts too. And ball caps. Another man'll be along selling that directly. There, see?"

He did. A man wearing a blue ball cap and tee-shirt with the Finger front and center was handing out ball caps and tee-shirts and collecting dollars.

Sirens wailed.

A half dozen cop cars sped toward them on the dirt shoulder of the gravel road, raising clouds of dust.

"They's coming in droves now," shouted the man. "Yesterday, she was nothing up to this!"

The traffic kept turning into the mammoth dirt lot of the Finger.

A man held a megaphone. "Hear, hear, hear! The cops are coming. Stand your ground. This is private property, owned by Finger Incorporated! Stand your ground!"

Cops, two apiece, were exiting cop cars.

They were burly guys, with big heads—and helmets. Batons swung from their black-gloved fists.

"Watch yourself!" yelled the man. "They's a bunch of badasses. Watch yourself!"

The crowd moved like waves of water to the beat of the cops' boots. Cops whacked their batons against their black-gloved palms.

When the crowd parted, Peter got a flash glance at the base of the Finger. Look at that wide palm and those nails dangling down!

But then the frantic mob scattering obscured his vision.

"Here she goes!" cried the man. "Looks like she's going to be a bad one. Ain't she?" He tugged at Peter.

Several cops burst into the crowd. Wails, shrieks, painful cries.

A bullhorn: "Disperse!"

A man with a megaphone shouted back: "This is the property of Finger Incorporated! You're on private property!"

"No permit!" yelled the bullhorn. Another cop with a bullhorn marched in step with the first cop with his bullhorn. "Disperse. You're *unauthorized*. This site is *unauthorized*."

"It's in litigation," shouted the man with the megaphone.

"You!" shouted the first cop with the bullhorn. "Put that horn down. You are not authorized."

"Shove it up your ass!" shouted the man with the megahorn.

The cop with the bullhorn advanced quickly.

"God!" yelled out the man next to him. "Oh, dear God!" and Peter saw the man get whacked across the side of the head and his glasses hit the ground.

Peter grasped the top of his own head and ran hard. He ran headlong into a weedy, brushy field.

Something struck his head. He yelped in pain. He saw it as it ricocheted off into the weeds and scrub. He went to investigate, holding the back of his head. One of those miniature fingers. He leaned over, grabbed it, and ran with it.

He went for the woods.

Bullhorns.

He went in deeper, stumbling, rustling the underbrush.

Shots rang out.

He ran hard, stumbling, falling, getting up, running, stumbling.

What if they shot him? What if they did? And yet what had he done but show up?

Panic rose wet in his throat, and his chest heaved.

Because this was the real thing, wasn't it?

This *was*.

Nothing was ever as real as this—never.

His head hurt. Would they do him more damage?

He lay low a few hours with his back to the trunk of a huge tree before he attempted to stir, to rise, stand up and make his way, creep, to the edge of the woods—peer about, get his bearings.

Activity diminished.

It *looked* safe.

It *sounded* safe.

The crowd gone now, the cop cars gone, a few scattered hangers-on milling about the Finger.

Ah. He made his way slowly, step by step, through the weeds and scrub.

His head was feeling better. It was no longer throbbing.

Back in the camp now, and at the base of the Finger.

Now, finally.

He approached, and came up close. He might now encounter it directly.

He paused a moment, and then began running his hand over the rough concrete.

This was the base of the palm, wrinkled. Look at this, such nice etching, such fine tool work. He paraded along the palm, noticing, up higher, the well-defined palm lines and wrinkles.

Fifty feet or more, this palm spanned. Yes, surely.

He went to the middle.

Then he looked down, bent over, and got down on his knees. Ah, the wide stub of a wrist, jutting up, supporting the palm.

What fine verisimilitude!

He stood up, and looked straight on.

And then moved back just a little and looked up again.

Three fingers folded down, index finger, ring finger, pinky, each descending from twenty feet high or more, over this concrete palm facing him.

And look at the fine precision of those nails. One had to admit. One *did* have to admit, didn't one?

And that thumb up there, bent over the index and ring fingers.

Such remarkable craftsmanship:

Nails, knuckles etched in concrete.

Credit was in order, wasn't it?

Something to wonder at?

He'd been aware of someone nearby, and even heard a murmur and wheezy breathing, a cough, but so fixed was his attention on the palm and fingers that he couldn't take a moment away—but now, there was an insistent nasal twang that broke his thoughts.

"Whatcha up to, there, fella?"

"Plenty," said Peter. "There's plenty to cogitate on here."

"What's that?"

"Leave me alone—for a minute or more."

"Sure, buddy. Don't wanta pester a man. Go ahead. Look. Lookin's free."

Peter backed away a good ten feet.

He bent his head back and looked up as high as he could.

What upthrust!

A palpable presence here!

The Rich Man had to know that this was vast denigration.

He told the man with the nasal twang.

"Rich Man? Hell, he's about a mile over thataway—on that

blacktop, Route B, is where he is. Only you won't be able to get on the man's property if that's what you're a-thinking. They's tried, but paid for it."

"How so?"

"You can drive by if it suits you. Only I wouldn't get out and look none."

"I won't," said Peter.

He found his car where he'd left it.

His car had a deep dent in the hood.

A sticker was stuck behind the windshield wipers. "No parking," the sticker said. "Pay fine at Whump County Court House."

He drove off, raising dust.

He turned onto Route B.

Rich Man.

It was time to see the Rich Man.

Or rather, his spread.

He drove past the woods where'd he'd hidden himself away, in fear, and finally came to some rolling pasture land, and then he spotted it—he saw it looming ahead.

It rose out of the hilly land like a rebuke.

A mansion five, or was it six, stories high?

He got nearer.

Six.

Nothing agricultural here, no cows, no pigs, no sheep.

No farm buildings.

Rich green lawns—at least what he could see over the walls and gates.

Astroturf?

It didn't look real.

A white marble mansion.

Oh my, what beauty! What absolute . . . *beauty.*

But the Finger, the Finger?

The pale moon had risen above it.

He couldn't seem to come to the end of it.

He clocked it.

Quarter mile, half mile.

Rambling, palatial, windows winking light into the incipient darkness.

Now *this* was a house. Or could you call it a house?

Castle?

Palace?

He did a U-turn and went back to look, to take it all in—or at least what he *could* take in, driving by.

He stopped about midpoint.

He pulled along the side of the blacktop, across the road from it, and got out of his car. He stood looking.

Now just feast your eyes on that.

My, my, but this kind of immensity does have its appeal.

And then he heard them.

Harsh reports like doors slamming.

Shots—those were shots.

He got back in the car in a hurry and sped off. He leaned low against the steering wheel.

Would it be his head this time? Would it be between the eyes?

21

"I ran."

"Ran? From whom?"

"Cops. With batons. Advancing, beating, moving in for the kill."

"Then what choice did you have?"

"Most of them held their ground."

"Most. But not you? How does that make you feel?"

"Not good. An apostate."

"I can't blame you, really."

He told her about hiding in the woods. Deep in, behind a huge oak. He felt unsafe, even there. But he feared getting lost. He could go no further. This was good enough—better than out there, against the cops. Really, who wanted to be slaughtered by those nightsticks?

"There's nothing gained by cops beating heads," said the Assistant Dean. "It's best to use the pen, which, I'd like to remind you, is mightier than the sword."

The Assistant Dean relying on a cliché?

Yet it made him feel better. She bandaged his head.

"Flush that Finger out of your head and get back to your book. That would be most productive, wouldn't it?"

"Good advice. But at least I've seen the Finger. I've seen it. It was . . . it was inexpressible."

"How so?"

"I'm searching for a word," he said.

"Oh?"

"Yes. You would have to be there. To see it firsthand . . . shocking, Faustian, more than concrete, more than—"

"Yes?"

"Which way is up, which down? Maybe it's the act of leaning back so far that you lose . . . perspective."

"Well," she said. "But that's over. Now it's on to the book for you. And I wish you well."

"It must be," he said, "at the heart of my book."

"Oh, Peter. Such a coarse and tasteless thing as that?" She shook her head. "Really, I think not."

"But vital. Crude but vital."

"A central icon? No, I don't think so. Perhaps relegated to a subordinate icon?"

"No—*central*. A metaphor for the age. *And* for the timeless!" He took down the miniature finger from the bookshelf. He held it up.

"Well, it's your project, but if it were *I*, really, I would choose a loftier subject."

"Icons of power tend to be raw and rough: rack, spiked iron ball, thumb screws. Meditate on those."

"I'd rather not," she said. "But if you must use these, then find some balance. Between the sacred and the profane. Make it grandiloquent, august!"

He nodded. Of course he would.

But he struggled with it. As he dug into it, he began to feel, more and more, the coarseness of his icon. There was nothing collegial about this Finger. It was in your face rude and raunchy. But Rich Man's white marble . . . *ah, such* . . . *such* . . . and yet the Finger, he couldn't give it up. He mustn't.

"Well," said Lucinda Marigold, "perhaps I could provide a welcome balance. If you must keep that particular icon."

"How is that?"

"Poetry. A spot here, a spot there."

Poetry?

Had she intended this all along?

"Well, maybe."

"Look. Let me show you," the Assistant Dean said. "Give me the Image." She had come to call it that—*the Image*.

He handed her the miniature. There was still a speck of blood in the delicate lines of the finger, near the knuckle joint.

"All yours," he said.

She held it up. "Observe this," she said, "as I read."

He prepared himself.

Her voice was sonorous, full-bodied, the imagery delineating this very Finger, this Image, but giving it a sacrosanct quality he couldn't quite have imagined. He heard Wagner and Chopin combined. He found himself meditating on the Finger thrust before him as the ethereal domain of all abstraction.

"Are you listening? Did you hear me?" she asked, shaking him.

"What?" He looked up.

"Did you fall asleep? Jeez, I hope it wasn't that boring."

"No. No. It was . . . mesmerizing. It was transporting."

"You were charmed? You were seized?"

"Yes—charmed, seized. Indeed I was."

"They *never* like my stuff," she said. "But I will do it anyway. I will forge on—and on."

"The Finger," he said. "As you read, I saw it . . . in a different light."

"You did? Was it beautiful?"

"Yes, it was—the very essence of the Finger. I saw it . . . for the first time. The anger, the resolve, the poetic justice—they were all there!"

Or maybe it was just the fine poetry. Though maybe that was just the passion of her voice, the ways she sounded out the vowels, the slippery tongue, her lisp that turned him on.

He moved toward her.

"Oh, I'm so happy," she said. "Let's eat."

22

H is phone rang.

"You've had plenty of time now," said Shelia. "I said to myself—just wait. See if he remembers. But *no*, I guess you didn't."

"Work," he said. "Lots of work."

"But you've given it some thought? Some serious thought?"

"Some."

"I hope so. I do hope so. I've got a little surprise for you. I'll soon be on my way! I'm coming straight to your apartment this weekend, Peter. So be ready!"

He jumped. "Here? This—"

"This weekend, dearest."

"But—"

"Prepare well for me—stock up your fridge!"

He started to object, but she was gone.

She's closing in, he thought. Is there any resisting her?

He told the Assistant Dean about it over wine that evening.

"*She*?"

"Old friend."

"Well, I won't be here. You can count on that. But I did want to tell you, I've given it some thought, and I've decided to move in with you."

"Move in?"

"You don't want me to?"

"Sure."

"Not a *sexual* thing, Peter. Merely Platonic. Is that clear?"

"Why?"

"Well, perhaps I'd better not."

He said nothing.

"Maybe we ought to give it a little time," she said. "I just thought we could work better being closer together. Get the book done. Work around the clock. You see? Put it in high gear!"

He imagined it. Maybe it would start Platonic, then develop? Worth a shot.

But would it be the same? There wouldn't be the expectation, the waiting for Lucinda Marigold to pull open the exterior door, take the stairs, the sound of her shoes in the hall, the three hard knocks on the door. The shoe sounds would be different, more knowing. She wouldn't knock but stick a key in and let herself in. She would come in, head into their common bedroom, drop her purse there and remove her shoes there—not in the living room.

"There's a reading this Friday," she said, "before your *girlfriend* shows up. We should go."

"Reading by whom?"

"Olivia Fuchia, a woman who's won some sort of poetry award. I don't particularly want to hear her read, but I'd like to find out what's so special about her. I can just imagine. Can't you?"

"Imagine what?"

"The stale air of predictability. The vacuous. The language grounded in the quotidian. Desires, feelings, the intensely personal."

"What's she written?"

"*Sister Love.* We'll see. Won't we?"

"What?"

"How worthy she is of this award."

23

"A new development," said the Assistant Dean, the next evening, "in liaisons." He was to meet with Major George Griper the following morning. "Now, that's not pronounced the way it looks," said the Assistant Dean. "He called me this morning, and said that the *i* is a short vowel sound—so be sure to call him Major *Grip-per*. That seems very important to him, but then can you blame the man?"

"No," said Peter. "I sure can't."

The Major was a short, heavyset man with thick jowls. He licked his lips. "I'm a morning person, Professor. Here, let's tank up on some coffee and a few donuts. What do you say?"

"Good."

The Major held his gut. "You bet it's good! Outstanding!" He pointed at the coffee pot. "Get you a cup." He pointed at the donuts. "Grab a few!"

Peter did.

"Me—I eat too many donuts. You?"

"Not generally."

"Way too many." The Major patted his gut. "And say— just so we're clear about something. It's Major *Grip-per*. You were told, weren't you?"

"Yes. Grip-per."

"Outstanding. You wouldn't believe, Professor, the hell I've caught since I turned Major. Know what I mean?"

"Sure."

"It was actually better when I was Captain. Not that I'd want to go back to *that*, of course. Less responsibility. Less pay."

"Definitely."

"But what's it going to be like if I get to General? *General Gri-per*? Now how's that going to sound? Huh? What do you think?"

"Not good."

"Nobody likes a griper. *Live* with it. Suck it up. You know the drill. And especially a military man. You know?"

"Right," said Peter.

"Now *Colonel* Griper doesn't sound too bad."

"No."

"But then who wants to stay put at that if you could go for the gold? Huh?"

"You wouldn't want to—of course not."

The Major leaned in close to him. "I *long* to be General Gripper, Professor. You know that? It's been a lifelong ambition—from my earliest remembered days of childhood. It's been a dream! Oh, how we humans *dream*. But what would life be without that Great Dream? Huh?"

"Yes, yes. Important. Very important."

"Professor Boatz, huh? I'll bet you get *your* share. I'll just bet you do. Boats. Ships. Canoes. That sort of thing?"

"No—not really."

"No? Well, *damn*. I would've thought. Well, be that as it may, here we are—the two of us, you and me, to talk about icons. I was told you're into icons of power. I like that. I like that very much."

"You do?"

"Very much."

"Well, at present I am. I'm all about icons of power," said Peter.

"Outstanding! Then we have something in common." The Major raised his coffee cup. "I've got a whole setup—come. Come, take a look." He winked. He motioned for Peter to follow.

They carried their coffee and donuts.

They entered a spacious room.

A gigantic table covered with green felt was filled with miniature Army men, tanks, troop carriers, jets, and all kinds of military equipment.

The Major laid a hand on his shoulder. "Look. Absorb."

Peter's eyes roamed about. It was hard to lock on to one single thing here. It was all so ... so *what*? So thorough? So multitudinous?

"What do you think?"

"Lots of—"

"Things, aren't there? Comes from a factory outlet. From a toy manufacturer, but tell me, does this look like something for kids?"

"Well . . ."

"Does it, though? Huh?" The Major bit into a doughnut, ripping off a hunk like a dog after a piece of creaturely flesh.

To Peter, this vast array before him passed for an Army man bonanza. What a kid wouldn't give for this! He ambled about, gazing, touching. Here was a city being bombed. Here, a city besieged. Such verisimilitude!

"In a way," said Peter, "it announces to me—*kids*. Depending, of course, on how you look at it."

"Maybe it does, in a way," said the Major, chewing. "But what's wrong with that?"

"Nothing, I suppose."

"Each of these scenarios *is* an icon, isn't it?" The Major sipped coffee.

Peter hesitated.

"Do say I've got a few icons here, Professor. Hell, lie to me!" He laughed and banged Peter on the shoulder.

Peter took a bite of doughnut.

"Which icon?"

"I'd hoped *you* could tell me."

"Me?"

"You're a professor of icons."

"That's true."

The Major pointed. "That, for instance."

"That—"

The Major escorted him to the thing in question.

"Now *here's* a weapon to be reckoned with. Huh?" The Major fingered it.

Peter studied this thing in question. It was a battlewagon of some sort, colored in Army camouflage.

"My own contraption," said the Major. "This thing can deliver a payload not just from one angle or two, or three. No, this thing can fire at *three-sixty*." He grinned big. He set his coffee cup down on the table, between a troop carrier and a jet plane. Coffee slopped out on the green felt table cover. "What do you think? What do you think about that?"

"Three-sixty?"

"Affirmative. Think back now. The wagon train being circled? Recall that?"

"Yes."

"With this, Professor, the wagon train sprays away at all angles!" He grabbed up his cup, slopping out more coffee. "Now what's the *icon*?   Pin it down for me. What *are* we talking about here, sir?"

"Death, destruction, mayhem?"

The Major stepped back. "Well, yes, outstanding! But where does this thing fit?"

"Fit?"

"With the rest of it?"

"The rest? As in?"

The Major shook his head. "I don't get it," he said. "I'm a thinking man, Professor, and I don't get it. Sure, it's death, destruction, and mayhem, but what else? What else *is* it? Is that *all* it is because I would hate to think—"

"I don't know," said Peter. "What else could it be?"

"You're the professor," said the Major. "Surely you've thought about these matters."

"Well," said Peter. "Let's start with what we know." It was a typical teaching tool for his undergrad classes.

"Outstanding."

"What *do* we know?"

"It shoots at three-sixty."

"Good. What else?"

"It kills everything within a quarter-mile range."

"And?"

"It pierces traditional plated armor coating on any tank you can imagine."

"And?"

"Has a flame thrower function."

"And?"

"Runs without refueling for thirty-six hours."

"Has the machine been built?"

"No."

"Will it be built?"

"Let's assume it will."

"You're seeking a patent?"

"Maybe."

"What is its purpose? Its function?"

"Get the job done."

"What job?"

"The job we're given."

"Who's given?"

"Military."

"For what?"

"What? Freedom."

"It's an icon of freedom?"

The Major fingered it. "I guess that's what it is. It's an icon of freedom. Damn straight!" He grabbed Peter's hand. He shook it hard. "Thanks. Thank you, Professor!"

The Major moved in for a hug.

Peter started to go.

"The higher-ups, you know. You have to fill out these . . . these justifications. This, this—what you just helped me see—this is good. *Very* good."

The Major gave him a big bear hug.

Peter felt tears spring to his eyes.

Damn! Why'd that have to happen?

"Another donut?"

"Thanks."

Peter stayed around for two more.

24

The room was crowded. Olivia Fuchia introduced herself, spoke of her poetry award, thanked the awards committee, and spoke of growing up, her favorite authors, her loves. *Sister Love* came out of all that, she said, a need to find core values in sisterhood. How are we centered? Where do we go wrong? What is the special bond between sisters, a bond that can be broken if not carefully tended to?

She introduced her first poem, "Regrets," a poem dealing with sisterly quarrels.

He noticed Lucinda's frozen grin. Grim, actually—malevolent, even. She sustained that grin for the entire forty minutes of the reading. He looked momentarily at her, now and then, and yes—there it was. Frozen like a manikin's plastic lips.

They filed out through a thick line of professors and students crowding the aisles heading to the podium where the author stood before a stack of thin blue books.

"Damn it," shouted Lucinda on the way to the car, "sisterhood! Can you believe it! She writes about sisterhood. Consider, Peter, the nature of the world. Consider all the people starving, bombed, tortured, and she writes about sisterhood? Sisterhood? Is there not a mightier calling for literature?"

"Maybe that's all she knows," offered Peter.

"Know more then!" shouted Lucinda. "I need a drink."

They headed to a bar.

"We need a lofty subject for all discourse. Or keep our mouths shut. I firmly believe it." She was half soused by now. "Keep your fucking mouth shut unless you can elevate your platform to the mystical reaches of the gods themselves, to Mount Olympus. Do you get what I'm saying, Peter? Really, do you?" She placed a tentative hand on his arm.

"Yes—I think so. Of course I do." He did not want to tell her that he rather liked the poetry of Olivia Fuchia, that it had a ring to it that was pleasing to his ears. And that, at one point, he had visualized the two sisters on a swing in the backyard and had felt the tears come to his eyes as they had waited for a fudge bar to be delivered by their mother, an everyday sort of woman who loved to make her two daughters feel special. It had a sweet, wistful quality to it that moved him in mysterious ways. And he could taste the fudge bar—that's what surprised him.

"Get *this*," said Lucinda, that malicious grin reappearing. "Listen. Imagine a man being thumbscrewed. Imagine the screws being tightened. He yelps in pain. Imagine his despair, knowing full well there is no hope, that he is absolutely at the mercy of this hooded monster who won't let up, who will only tighten the screws until he confesses to something he did not do, nor even has a clue about, not knowing in the least what to confess. Imagine now, you read one of those poems to him. Imagine, in that chamber of horrors, that you read the poem about playing chopsticks together on a Sunday morning. Remember that one?"

Yes—he did. It stuck out even more than the swing and fudge bar one. There they were, two cute little girls, age twelve and thirteen, sitting on the piano bench together on a bright June Sunday morning, plinking away on the Grand piano, and in the other room mother and father doing the breakfast dishes, and outside: the fresh thick, dewy green grass, and the yellow dandelions. Green and yellow, yellow and green, brightness, beauty, an airy lightness and the plinking piano as bright and as light. Yes, he remembered it. It too had brought tears to his eyes.

"Now, then," said the Assistant Dean, sloshing her glass of wine, "I want to invite you to consider this poor hapless creature with his two thumbs in the process of being mangled. Let's read *this* poem to him. Let's serenade him with *this* poem and see what he says!"

The waitress arrived. "Refill?"

"Sure," said Lucinda. "You bet—Peter?"

"Of course."

"Now, where were we? Well, Peter, I need not say much more on this point. Really, need I? Is this a mighty enough theme? Is this fitting to the seriousness of the world we live in? The darkness, the utter malevolence seeping through the human species like pestilent waters?"

"But," he said, "the piano notes, the fresh green grass, and the yellow dandelions."

"They would cheer the man with the thumbscrews?"

"Nothing would cheer the man with the thumbscrews," said Peter.

"Listen to me," she said. And she spoke of the Finger, of the right kind of poetry, and though she had felt, when she had read it before, that something rich and august transformed this ordinary— who could deny it: *obscene*—thing to the universal, she did feel that the poetry needed to be more mixed: a combo of the transcendent and the utterly pedestrian. "If," said Lucinda, "we see that unholy alliance in the poetry itself, the essence itself becomes more clear— by stark contrast."

This last word came out *conchast*.

"All to the good," Peter noted.

"I'm going to be sick," said Lucinda. "Let's go home."

"Sorry, sorry."

Later she said, "Well, I do feel better."

"Coffee?" he said.

25

The Assistant Dean had cleared out.

It was best. There was the issue of jealousy, of course.

"Oh, so . . . *here's* where you live." Sheila dropped her suitcase on the living room floor.

"Why the suitcase?"

"Because I'm staying."

"But—"

"No *buts*, Peter."

"Listen," he said. Would they co-habit this very evening? He was half glad, half worried. When would the Assistant Dean return?

She looked around. "Living room—I might have expected all these books and papers." She peered in the kitchen. "Not very big—pretty small, actually, but I guess it'll have to do. For a while, at least." She came back and looked into the bedroom. "Well, it looks big enough. At least, *that's* big enough." She peered into the bathroom. "Pretty small, but I can get ready, I guess, in that rather limited space. What's for lunch?"

"Maybe we'd better go out."

"I told you'd I'd be hungry." She pulled open the refrigerator. "Not much in here. What *do* you eat?"

She stood facing him—as though studying him for signs of something. "Man Two is no go. I'm marrying you, Peter. It's not like we don't already *know* each other—in the Biblical sense. After all, we must have *known* each other a million times—before. So . . . I'm claiming what is rightfully mine: you." She took his hand.

"I'm not exactly set up right now," he said, "for this."

"Oh? How so? It's big enough. I'll put up with it."

"I'm going to be living with someone."

"What? You might have told me. Who?"

He explained.

"Well. That's nice and cozy."

"Platonic."

"Don't be stupid. She just said that. Don't be gullible."

"Intellectual," he said. "That's the extent of it."

"And let's say it is. How does that work for you? Don't you have needs—*other* needs? What a silly question. Of course you do. I of all people know *that*."

She paced the floor. "Well, you choose. Go ahead. I don't think there's much of a choice, though. But if you wait too long, you're going to end up with nothing—or something pretty weird. I can give you something good, something that'll last."

"But—"

"But what?"

"There's this other woman, you see."

"As you just mentioned."

"Yes."

"Go ahead," she said. "You make your bed."

She left.

In a huff.

26

He was writing around the clock now, and Lucinda Marigold was there to witness it. In the dark wee hours, she would head to the kitchen, pull open the refrigerator door, and take out a glass of ice cold water. He saw her from his living room work space. She stood there observing him as she drank. He was to do the framing up, the prose, she the poetry. His title: *The Finger: A Summative Icon of Power*. It seemed to suggest the augustness and grandiloquence that Lucinda Marigold was calling for. Her dark trips to the refrigerator felt like the goddess of transcendental forms bearing witness to his tireless efforts. And they *were* very hard. He was exhausting himself. He was *reaching*. He was trying to muster up all he could in defense of the Universal Idea, as Lucinda termed it.

But something continued to trouble him. It was gross, wasn't it, that Finger? Crude—and yes, *obscene*?

And yet, that fine art work, those precise details of wrinkles and lines in the concrete flesh—well, that was artistry, was it not?

And redemptive in ways?

He could not decide—completely.

"What is it all worth," the Assistant Dean said one morning, "if it's not published? It *must* be published. A writer must have an audience. If you have no audience, then you have only yourself—alone. This is a solipsistic trap."

He was about to respond when she said, "The cat. I haven't seen it forever."

Nor had he.

"I haven't heard it below," she said. She left the apartment, key in hand. He heard her on the stairs. He heard her stop at the bottom landing. The outside door didn't open.

He heard feet move. He heard her steps up the stairs, outside the door, and then the key in the lock.

"Well," she said, "I don't know. I haven't seen the cat. Where, oh where, is the little darling, do you think?"

"Probably we've just missed him," said Peter. "After all . . . all the work, all the exhaustion."

"Not *me*," she said. "You, you've worked. You poor darling. But where in hell's the cat?"

She sat down and held her face in her hands. "If anything, anything has happened at all to that cat, I will never forgive myself!"

"What?"

"I feel that way," she said, "however odd it may sound to you. I do distinctly feel that way."

"Why?"

"Because, you see, I knew about it. I marked it down in the interstices of my being, and in that way, I claimed it. And I should have been watching. I should have noted its comings and goings, its breathings and purrings, all its cat ways."

"How could you have done that?"

"I couldn't have, of course. I'm only exaggerating to make a point."

"And what point is that?"

"That when you make a claim on another being, whatever that being is, call it Being, capital B, when you do this, Peter, it becomes a metaphysical liaison of You, capital Y, and Other, capital O. You see, we enter a circle of Being in which we suffuse the fullness of our *own* being, like circulatory blood, like water pumping through plumbing pipes, like electrical circuits, with *Otherness*. We become one Self, capital S, Peter. No longer Self and Other. We are united in Love, capital L. Quantum theory tells us we exchange energy with each other. Where do you end and I begin? Our corporeal bodies are wide spaces, they tell us. We are energy. Non-tactile, Peter. I should have been watching that cat in the spirit of Love. I *am* my Brother's Keeper."

New Age?

"How could you watch the cat every minute of its life?"

"Watch it? I have no idea. We are charged with things which lay heavy, impossible burdens on us."

He let it rest.

27

His Project was finally complete. Ah yes, and what a terrible burden lifted.

He handed Lucinda the manuscript, an entire paper ream of it. She took it almost dispassionately—had she lost interest?

But apparently not. She stayed up into the wee hours night after night. He was exhausted and went to bed. But he found himself repeating her steps into the kitchen in the dark wee hours, getting a cold drink, eyeing her as she pored over the manuscript, and wrote on it. Like her, he said nothing. He went back into the bedroom and fell asleep after each moon-lit refrigerator trip.

"I read it five times," she told him.

She sat him down with the manuscript.

"Five times?"

"I'm a fast reader."

He awaited the grim news. "Yes?" He could see red ink-riddled pages as she turned them, one by one, and then sort of fanned them. "It's brilliant. It's *utterly* brilliant. You have written a work with great substance: You have left your mark on the world. Of course, some might argue that you would have been better off to have suffered yourself, and left some blood behind. But *I* do not argue this. In these pages I see oppression, suffering, despair. I see plague, infestation of murderous intent. And the Finger—ah, the Finger—how appropriate! You give it to all the oppressors, to all the tyrants. You give it to human existence *itself*—"

"Wait a minute," he said, "where do I do that?"

"It's implied. One must but read between the lines, Peter. It, the Finger, becomes sum and substance of the whole prospect of human existence. Its rank order of flesh, blood, and bone ground down to utter insignificance and cosmic laughter—the Finger obscenely gesturing at it all!"

"But then that means," he protested. "It means the work never quite reaches—"

"Oh but it does, certainly it does. That which is defilement due to oppression . . . and those who, in their ignorance, support this very oppression . . . both are unequivocally redeemed by the fact, Peter, that beyond all this is Spirit, capital S, though it's horrifying to think of the tainting we see in the material expression of this. The poetry does much to untaint the tainting, though, don't you think?"

"I hope so," he said.

"We've got a winner, Peter."

We, he thought. But *he* wrote most of the book. The poems were recycled. But, he thought, she did serve as grand inspirer—worth a considerable amount when one reflected on the prospect of facing publication alone.

"I would think," she said, "that the cover image should certainly be the Finger. Don't you think?"

"Uh, yes," he said. He imagined it.

Perhaps . . . but perhaps not.

"But we can't worry about that now. She took hold of his hand. "An agent," she said. "Of course we need an agent."

He nodded. Of course they probably would.

"For the thinking person," she said, "that's who this book is for. All the thinking people out there who want to *critically understand.* Understand what? The Finger in all its manifestations, its multiple meanings."

She knew a woman agent. A friend of a friend of a friend. This woman, it turned out, agreed to meet with both of them for lunch the following Friday.

"That soon?"

"She's reading the manuscript right now—the whole thing, Peter."

"I hope she likes it."

"Get your credit card out," she said, drawing hers out from her purse.

They scheduled flights.

She took off a couple days from her assistant dean work.

They were now landing, gathering their baggage, and soon in the limo on the way to the hotel.

"Yes, Peter—yes," said Lucinda, "she'll go for it. It's a wonderful, *wonderful* book. A beautiful brew of the social, the political, the philosophical, the poetic! Both of us at the top of our writing game. Don't you think?"

He hoped so. He hoped desperately that this was true.

"We swing this, and it's a new life for us, Peter." She took hold of his hand.

Now they were on their way in a cab to the fine restaurant where the meeting with the agent, Shirl Findley, was supposed to soon take place.

In exactly an hour and a half.

Shirl Findley, they'd discovered, was actually a third-stringer, or even fourth-, in the agency, but she had landed one book, though it hadn't sold very well. But she was at least in a pretty good agency. It wasn't a bad agency. Lucinda had her down as one with clout. "Not a lot of clout, but the way I read her, *some* clout. And clout, that's what we need—all the clout we can get."

They checked into the hotel.

"Our time is limited," said Lucinda. "To the restaurant— pronto!"

They came to the restaurant, paid the cab fare, plus tip. "We're over an hour early," said Lucinda. "We've got some time to kill, don't we?"

They walked about. They came to a bookshop a few blocks away.

"Yes!" said Lucinda. "Let's go in there. We'll check to see what's hot, what's not."

They spent a half hour browsing. "I don't see anything quite like our book," said Lucinda. "That tells you something."

"What?"

"I do feel hopeful, Peter. I really do."

She bought a few books of poetry on what she deemed a whim and handed him a philosophical work on the nature of blood. "I do think this might be nice to look at," she said. "Like yours, in ways."

He looked at the back panel. *Blood is the circuitry of consciousness. Anything with blood has consciousness.*

"How could you dispute it?" he said.

"What?"

"Nothing."

"She patted his hand. "I'll buy that for you."

They checked out. It was now thirty minutes until the meeting.

"We'd better go," he said.

"I think so."

When they were seated in the restaurant, he wanted wine but realized this would not be the appropriate time to order. You should order together, the three of you. But Lucinda said don't let agents push you around. She ordered wine, and when he hesitated, she ordered wine for him too.

"This is nice," she said. "I'm feeling very good about this."

They drank their wine, sat and waited. The time came, went, but no Shirl Findley. It was twenty minutes beyond when she was supposed to show. And so they waited longer. "It's times like these," said Lucinda, "I could smoke. You need something to keep you busy. Something to do with your hands."

The waitress appeared and poured more wine.

He was beginning to get a buzz on.

"You know what?" said Lucinda. "I'm about ready to call that bitch." She rummaged in her purse. "She treats us this way?"

And then he saw a tall, slim woman with flaming red hair. The waitress was pointing their way.

The woman was soon heading their way. Lucinda and he rose at the table.

"Oh, I am *so* sorry," said Shirl Findley. "I got in such traffic on the way here, and well . . . I am so, so sorry. How long have you been waiting?"

"Not that long," said Peter, shaking her hand.

When he finished Lucinda was shaking the woman's hand. There wasn't a hint of animosity in her now. She was all smiles and graciousness. The three of them sat down. The waitress arrived and they ordered. More wine poured, and Shirl Findley sat forward. "I read it. I like it." She wore a look of interest mixed with apprehension. He heard the *but* as plainly as he heard the *like it.*

"And?" said Lucinda.

He wished she hadn't been the one to say this. Shouldn't he, the writer, be the one to say this?

"Well," said Shirl, and she looked directly at Peter. "I read it, I like it, it's great. In fact there is so much about it that I do like so very much. Really, I do."

"I'm so glad."

"It has it all. It has the Grand Narrative, as you wrote in your email. It's so . . . totalizing. As you said. That may not work for some, but for many of our readers . . . well, I think it would work. They want totalizing. I suspect they do. The arc of the book is well-earned. I do believe it's well-earned. Yes, I think it is. And the examples drawn from history distilled with care and ordinary human feeling, pleasure and pain. There's a lot of pain in it. But pain is the thing we all experience. All of us. Don't we? Isn't that right?"

"And?" said Lucinda. "And?"

"Yes, of course," said Peter. "We all experience pain."

"It's important—pain is. The pain of ordinary circumstance— of ordinary life experiences, realizing that there are such larger pains we will never know. And so much drawn from the past, the terrible, terrible lives those people lived! Why, it just gives you—"

"The Finger," said Lucinda. "What about the Finger?"

"Ah, of course." Shirl Findley seemed to be choking up.

"Are you all right?" said Lucinda.

Concern? Yet he could detect malice festering in her cheeks, the way they were tightening on the smile lines.

"Yes—I'm all right. I'm just fine. I'm . . . I've been feeling, well kind of sad lately, and I think this wasn't exactly the time to read this book. I'm an emotional kind of person, I'll be upfront about this. I'm very emotional. And this book, so dark, so—"

"Goddamn it," said Lucinda, "spit it out. Are you interested or not? What about the poetry? Did you read the poetry?"

Shirl Findley jolted back in her seat. She collected herself, studied her hands. "Oh, I'm *so* sorry. I'm really very interested—for myself. But I don't know if a publisher would be interested. If you could ever get it by a publication committee. I'm just not sure of that."

"But you'll represent Peter. Correct?"

"Yes—well, it would depend."

"Depend? On what?"

Peter wanted to shut her up. This was his business, not hers. He'd written most of the book. All that about the Finger. Pages and pages of it. Its iconic value. Its contextual meaning. Its potential to shape the future. He moved in. "What would it depend on?"

"Changes. A lot of changes. Substantial changes."

"What kinds of changes?"

Shirl Finley pointed a finger at no one. She seemed to be directing the air. "It would have to be made more interesting in several ways—but to name one: The Finger must go. Or must be given more prominence. Reduce or expand. The philosophical might include it as a footnote. The political must give it preeminent concern. You have . . . a mixed breed."

"What?" said Peter.

"It would take some revamping and refocusing. And I'm not sure it's really worth it. I mean, who wants to read about . . . a finger? Who wants that image in mind? It's not hopeful. It's not upbeat. It's pretty . . . well, demoralizing."

"Oh, god," said Lucinda. She rose from the table. "Son of a bitch! That's the fucking point!" She sat back down. "And yet *note* the way the poetry gives it relief. Gives it new form and fine, grand resonance. Don't you *think*?"

Shirl Findley's lips trembled. "Well . . . maybe. I will have to admit, I didn't read the poetry all that carefully." She stared at them. "If you go with the political, which seems pretty thin, readers will want a toolkit for handling the oppression they face—or think they face?—from the rich and powerful. If that is, indeed, their real oppressor. They will want takeaways with clear and well-defined objectives. But I just don't see that here. I'm so sorry."

"Toolkit?" said Peter.

"Come on," said Lucinda, grabbing Peter's arm. "Let's go. We don't have to put up with this bullshit!"

Peter gave Shirl Findley a look, then shook her hand. And then he met up with Lucinda on the sidewalk.

"Are you thirsty?" she said. "I sure as hell am. I could drink a gallon. Of *hard* liquor—that is. And look over there. Bob's Tavern 1000. Neat name. You think he owns one thousand taverns? I like taverns. I like the name tavern. Don't you?"

"It suits me," said Peter.

"Oh, hell," said Lucinda. "She's such a foolish little person. We're better than that."

"She's not so little," he said.

"No—she had to be six feet tall."

They hurried across the street.

"Well, look," said Lucinda, "it's a fine, fine book the way it is. If no one wants it, screw them. And I mean it. Screw them!"

They sat in Bob's Tavern 1000 with scotch and bourbon.

Was Bob the guy at the bar? The man with large biceps and torso? The man with hair to his shoulders? The man with tattoos covering his neck and arms? He looked like he could rip your head off. Bartend and bouncer—owner too?

"Don't give up," said Lucinda. "We'll find a way to market it." She held her drink to her lips. "I can visualize it at the bookstore. I'm picturing it right now." She was looking toward the plate glass window with Bob's Tavern 1000 printed in large red letters, only backwards from this inside perspective.

"I won't do the toolkit," he said.

"Of course you won't. We'll try another agent. We've still got time." She drank down several gulps of scotch and shoved the short glass ahead of her. "We're here. Let's make the most of the opportunity."

"Don't we need an appointment?"

She motioned at the bartender. "More, please." He came with the bottle, refilled hers, then started to refill Peter's. But Peter shook his head.

"Skip the fucking agent. You know what we're going to do?

146

We're going to streamline the process, and march right into a publisher's office. And we're going to pitch our book right there. That's what we're going to do. That's the way it used to be, didn't it? Didn't it used to be that way? I mean you see movies, and so forth, and wasn't it like that?"

"I guess so."

"You guess."

"It was that way. To an extent, I guess."

"Well, that's what we're going to do. You know, Peter, the dean—Dean Chasm, that is, Dr. Dr. Dr. Chasm. I personally hate the bastard. I really do because he did nothing, absolutely nothing, to help me get my five books published. He could have got me in, see. He's published three himself—one on happiness. Did I tell you?"

"No."

He didn't mention he'd seen that purple happiness book. He didn't want to get into it.

"I thought I told you."

"I don't remember."

"You never listen to what I say. I think I *did* tell you. I'm almost sure I told you. Anyway, he's into this happiness stuff? For himself—not anyone *else*, like *me*. But anyway, he had me into his office for half an afternoon, spouting it, and of course, you know me, I'm pretty skeptical. I'm not one to swallow something as flabby as all that, but then I got to thinking, I *did* get to thinking, and really, really, Peter, I'm about to be a convert. I really *am*. If you say it, if you *speak* it, if you *believe* it—then you can will it into *existence*. That third book he published?"

"Yes?"

"Willed it into existence. Said he would publish it. Wouldn't take no for an answer! Wrote on the calendar: 'Day this book will come out.' It came out within a month of the date he wrote on the calendar. Now how's that for you?"

"Surprising."

"There's an icon for you!"

"What?"

"*What* what?"

"Which icon?"

"Oh, hell, I don't know. Hell, something...it would be something crystallizing the will to believe. Make it a tower, a skyscraper of human endeavor, a monolithic structure reaching up to the sky, the stars, the heavenly firmament. Triple the size of any skyscraper you can name or have ever seen. And I don't mean the fucking Finger! *That* would be an icon for *you*. And isn't that something, in an age of no belief—or should I say, the age that questions the very basis of belief—that we should have such belief? And why shouldn't we? Why, why?" She was looking around.

"What do you want?"

"Bob!" she shouted out.

The bartender turned toward her.

"I'm not Bob," he said. "But what's your pleasure?"

"A refill, please."

"Yes, ma'am."

The bartender came with two bottles and refilled Lucinda's with scotch, set that down, and grabbed up the bottle of bourbon and topped off Peter's glass.

"Oh, well," said Peter.

The bartender took off.

Lucinda drank a third of hers down in one gulp.

He feared for her.

"I see that look, she said. "I'm *prepping*. Sometimes you've got to prep yourself. Drink it down, Peter."

"Well," he said. But he drank his glass down slowly. He liked a buzz but not too much of a buzz.

"Oh, I know. You're not in the mood. But I'll get you in the mood. Want to go back to the hotel for . . . *a little afternoon of you know what?*"

God, he thought, what's happened? What's happened to this assistant dean?

He smiled.

"And then—but *no*, then it would be too late. No, we're going to first march right in, just as I said. We're going to march right in and demand it, Peter, *demand* to be heard. For one person, there, right there, sitting at some editorial desk, to take a look. And I mean *now*. Not two weeks, not three weeks, ten weeks, god, fifteen, twenty, thirty, fucking a hundred weeks! No, right on the spot! Look at it, a page or two, three pages—what's it to them? Come on, what's it to them?"

The bartender looked their way.

"It's their job," said Peter. "Their job. Like what if a student came to you and wanted immediate action on something that—"

"That's different. That's *not* the same at all." She stood up, swaying and then gripped the table with both hands.

"How so?"

"Oh, come on. Surely you see the difference."

"What is the difference?"

"Does a student put that much effort into anything? The answer is no. How much effort do we, as writers, put into our projects? Think what I'm saying. Consider."

This last came out as *con-shid-eer*.

"Well," he said, "I guess you have a point."

She beckoned at him with a bent finger. "You know I do. Let's get moving. Let's stop the jabber." She held up her cell phone and checked the time. "It's almost three. We can be there by three-thirty at the latest. At the latest, Peter." She slapped the table. "This is the day you take the place by storm. This is the day of the enormous white tower, Peter!"

"I'm ready," he said.

"Do you need help or something?" said Lucinda, taking him by the arm. She pulled him, swaying.

"No, I'm fine."

"Are you *sure*?"

"I'm okay."

"Well, then we need to hurry a little."

They scatter-walked toward the door, past the bartender, whose biceps were flexing.

Peter couldn't help but look at the tattoos. What were they? How were they connected?—if at all.

"Goodbye, folks. Come again."

"If we're in town, we will," said Lucinda. "You can bet on that. And I suspect from now on, we will be in town a bunch."

"Good for you." He gave them a little wave.

Lucinda stopped, just short of the door.

"Goddamn it, if we're going to get to the publisher in any kind of sensible time-frame," Lucinda said.

"What publisher?"

"I don't know! We'll look around." Then she said to the bartender, "Do you know where there's a publisher around here? A book publisher?"

"Book publisher . . . hell, I don't know." He looked confused, as though he'd been batted one in the forehead. "Wait a minute . . . it's coming to me. Yes. Two blocks over. I got hit on my hog there, and I know it's a book publisher because I looked up and what I saw was the name—I'm telling you. Saw the name right when the fucking— excuse me—when the goddamn car sideswiped me. But what was the name of that place? Let me think."

He laid a hand across his forehead.

"We're losing time," Lucinda said to Peter.

"Let me think. Let me think. Okay, it's *Book Palace*. Got all kinds of books in there. You can see them through the plate glass window."

"No!" said Lucinda, "that's a book*store*, not a book *publisher*. It's a *store*, where they sell books."

"That's where we were," said Peter.

"Yes, yes."

"Oh. Hell. Well, I only know I got rammed on my hog right in front of that damn place."

"Sorry," said Lucinda. "That's terrible. But thank you."

"Don't mention it."

They marched outside and walked a few buildings down.

"Wait a minute," said Lucinda. She leaned against a plate glass window of an antique store. "I don't know what's wrong with me. Check the web! Check the internet! Check Google! Check and get an address. What a fool I am. What a fool, fool, fool!"

She was coming undone, but in his own liquor fog, he didn't see it as a bad thing. "Okay," said Lucinda, shoving the cell phone at him. "Take a look. It's on Broadway. Davy Jones Books. Where are we now? Let me check. Let me check."

"This is Broadway. Isn't it?"

"Huh?"

"Isn't this Broadway?"

She stared at him. "Yes. This is Broadway. Of course." She whacked her forehead with her fist. "But where on Broadway? Where *are* we on Broadway?" She turned about and looked up.

"What?"

"Only a block away," she said. "Only a couple stupid blocks away, and we asked that clown in there."

"Wait a minute," said Peter. "We don't have the book with us."

She held up her cell phone. "They can read it off *this*, the bastards."

They entered the lobby of Davy Jones Books. Customer Service blocked off all entry.

"Yes, ma'am," said a woman dressed in a gray suit. "May I help you?"

"We're here to see an editor," said Lucinda.

"Editor? Do you have an appointment?"

"No."

"You would need an appointment to see an editor."

Peter noticed the name tag: Early Brown. What kind of name was *Early*? As a *first* name?

"Oh?" said Lucinda. "Is that right?"

Venom.

"What's your capacity? Are you an agent?"

"No, I'm not an agent," said Lucinda.

"I'm sorry, then," said Early Brown.

"Try," said Lucinda.

"Pardon?"

"Try and do," said Lucinda. "First you try, and then you do. This is a basic happiness principle." Words were slipping from her lips like eels.

"Pardon?"

"I've written five goddamn books, and I'm tired of it. This man here," she said, grabbing Peter roughly by the arm, "has written, with my co-authorship, a bestseller, but you think anybody cares? I'm tired of pipsqueaks like you keeping people like us from succeeding. You will not do that . . . act like a publisher, goddamn it!"

"Security," said the gray-suited woman, on the phone. There was a momentary pause. "Thank you."

Lock-up time, thought Peter. *Lock-up.*

"Fuck Security," yelled Lucinda, and she toppled so much she about hit her head on the Customer Service counter. He caught her. "Fuck Security. I want to see a publisher!"

Peter charged out of there.

Halfway down the block, he looked back.

Lucinda was running out of the building. Suddenly she stumbled and fell headlong on the sidewalk. She gathered herself up and continued running.

He ran for two blocks. He looked around to make sure he hadn't been followed. He hadn't except for Lucinda bringing up the rear.

"You abandoned me!" she shouted when she caught up with him.

"Sorry. But you were out of hand! Weren't you?"

"Maybe." She leaned against a building. "I'm tired. Full day. I want to rest. Let's go back."

"I'm hungry," he said.

"Yes," she said. "I'm hungry too."

It came to him: that proposed, potential afternoon love session, but he was afraid to mention it.

Tomorrow morning they'd be back on that plane.

This was sort of a vacation, wasn't it?

"Maybe," he said, "maybe we ought to . . ."

"What?"

"Nothing—nothing at all."

"Food," she said. "And drink. That's what I want."

PART THREE

THE FINGER

1

Sheila arrived again, this time with four suitcases and several boxes. She addressed Lucinda: "I've got prior claims on this man—which go way back. And so I'm moving in."

Lucinda packed up and left.

It was just him and her. And her stuff.

"Okay, let's see how this works," said Sheila. "I think we've got a good shot at this. I'm optimistic. When's your lease run out on this place?"

Peter examined his options. He'd been rereading his book. He'd been contemplating the Finger. It was a half mile high. Finger Two was now three quarters of a mile. Finger Three was a whole mile. He felt a great longing. He felt the pull of the thing.

His summer seminar was over.

Go to the Finger, he'd been thinking.

"Go *there*?" said Sheila. "Whatever for?"

"Something's pulling me. Such purpose. Such airy heights of the thing." Mountains called, didn't they? It was now the Finger calling. Didn't that make sense?

He took her by the hand. "Come with me," he said.

"Are you serious? Unequivocally no."

He got Lucinda on the phone. "No," she said. "You let her *oust* me."

"She willed the place into existence," said Peter. "For her."

"Don't use my own ideas against me," said Lucinda.

The phone went dead.

"I must go," said Peter. "It calls."

"I'm not staying here by myself," said Sheila. "That's not part of the bargain." She began carrying suitcases—out the door. He heard her feet clomping on the stairs.

He took off on his own. Five hundred miles. The motel was a relief. He set his alarm and popped up at six.

Coffee and doughnuts. He ate them on the way out to the

Finger.

A couple dozen trucks were parked in the huge dirt lot. A group of men and women with ball caps on were hanging about the base of the Finger like supplicants. Some were facing it, others leaning against it, leisurely smoking.

He made his way toward them and was welcomed with handshakes, hugs, and invitations for donuts and coffee.

He could use more.

He had grown hungry over the last few weeks.

The more food, the better. The more drink, the better.

"They're right over there," said a short grizzled man. "And grab you a ball cap. Right on that table over there—free tee-shirts there too, and literature."

A ball cap—in a new style: the image of the towering Finger against the blue sky but something distinctly different, scrawled in livid red: *The Finger Lives!* He grabbed a handful of brochures and got some coffee.

He returned to the assemblage of devotees.

"Now," said a gray-haired woman with a clipboard, "we need a couple folks to man the base—armed folks. Who's going to man the base? How about you, Ernest? You and Gene?"

"Sure," said Ernest. "Sure. I'm your man."

"Pieces are in the truck. Here's the key." She handed it to Ernest. "Don't shoot unless you have to. And don't shoot cops."

"Got it," said Ernest. He beckoned at Gene, a younger guy, with long, dirty blond hair.

"Bring me my weapon, okay?" said Gene.

Ernest stopped. He shook his head. "No. You come to the truck. You get your own weapon. Don't be lazy."

"Hell," said Gene. "I don't like this assignment to begin with."

"You want another assignment?" said the woman with the clipboard.

"Not really."

"You slacking on us today, Gene?"

"Hard night."

"Crow's Nest? All you had to do was look around, drink coffee, and talk to your girlfriend on your cell. How hard was that?"

"Yeah, and the damned fire—"

"*Shush,*" said the woman with the clipboard. She gave him a motherly pat on his shoulder. "*Shush.* We all have our problems."

"Come on, Gene," said Ernest. "Get your piece."

The woman with the clipboard said, "Now, who's watching the Perimeter? We need a half dozen or more cadre to watch the Perimeter."

A half dozen men raised hands.

"Yeah, good," said the woman with the clipboard. "Get your guns out of the truck." She raised a hand. "Now, don't go ballistic out there. Remember, you're protecting the property—that's it. That's all. Got it?"

"Anybody crosses that line," said an elderly man, "and he gets it right between the eyes."

The woman with the clipboard shook her head. "Go easy now."

"They's on the property," said another man, "and we got a right to defend ourselves."

The woman with the clipboard nodded.

"Now, then," said the woman. "We need a man on the Crow's Nest, and we need the rest of you walking the Outer Bounds. Who's on the Crow's Nest?"

The men and women looked about at each other. "Not me," said a woman with a stocking cap on. "I don't like heights."

"You don't like heights," laughed an old man with a long chin. "What's wrong with heights?"

"I'm scared. I get the flutters."

"You get the flutters."

"Well, hell, I ain't a-doing it," said a heavyset man in a red Finger tee-shirt. "I don't have room to move around up there. Why didn't you make the thing bigger?"

"I didn't have anything to do with that department," said the woman with the clipboard. "How about you?" she said to Peter. "You're new to it all. You'll get to know it up there. Know it *real* good. Won't he? No place like the Crow's Nest for understanding the Finger. Right?"

Several nods and assents.

"Crow's Nest?" said Peter.

She nodded, and then leaned way back and pointed up with a crooked finger. "Up *there*," she said, smiling. "See?"

"Up there?"

"Up there. Up there is *key*." She removed a sheet of paper from her clipboard. "Here's your duty sheet. Briefly you do three things: number one, scan the Outer Bounds; number two, scan the Perimeter; number three, update us on the Rich Man." She handed him a logbook marked *Rich Man*. He noticed the two columns: *Time* and *Activity*. A third of the log book had been filled. "Call me if you see any danger. Number's on the duty sheet."

He glanced at the sheet.

"You got a cell?"

"Yes—"

"Any questions?"

"No."

"You're—what's your name, sir?"

"Peter Boatz . . . Professor Peter Boatz."

"Professor Boatz, welcome aboard."

The others were at the truck. They were coming forth with weapons.

"Thanks."

She touched his arm. "Now, do be careful making your way up there. It's safe, but pay attention. Watch out for dizziness. I've got some pills for that."

He looked at the third duty: *Watch the Rich Man*. He pointed at it. "What's this about?"

"Your logbook there," said the woman. "Write down times and Rich Man activities. Anything that looks suspicious."

"As in—"

"Dangerous . . . just write down *any* activities—keep a log— and let us be the judge. Okay?"

"Yes."

He was getting jittery.

"Ready?"

He nodded.

"Follow me."

She guided him toward a table.

"Here's a thermos of coffee for you. Two sack lunches. Some pills, bottles of water. And a backpack to carry it all in. And, ah—a flashlight."

"Flashlight?"

"Yes, for the early hours. For getting down, Professor Boatz."

"Getting down? When is that?"

"At six in the morning, and it's still dark then, comrade."

"Why six?"

"Breakfast at seven sharp, then meeting."

She packed the backpack up for him. He hung it on his shoulder.

"Steps are right *that* way," she said. She shook his hand. "Do good work, comrade."

He headed the way she was pointing.

He rounded the base and saw the steps. He looked straight up. They wound around, up and around, like coils of a snake, and, if you leaned way back, you could see more and more coils, but not the very top. There was a halo of white cloud cover up there somewhere, sailing in the deep blue. He stared at the steps, and then took his first one.

"Be careful," said the woman with the clipboard. "Stop at the Crow's Nest, now. Don't go *all* the way up."

"Oh, no," he said.

But where was the Crow's Nest?

"You'll see it," she said. "There's several hi-tech viewers there, with high-powered lens."

He began his trip up—up.

One careful step at a time, a torturous turn, more careful steps. Up, up, up, step by step by step. Brace yourself. *Keep your attention on the steps—just the steps.* Now and then he had to adjust the backpack on his shoulders.

Finally, he stopped, took a rest, leaning against the concrete tower.

He saw it:

Rich Man's mansion.

Behold.

Do take note of this!

Spread out, oh my, rolling that three-quarters of a mile or so he'd seen from the road, but more—*oh, yes, more, so much more*—something he couldn't have imagined: how it rambled and rambled over the hills to the back until it disappeared out of sight, obscured by a screen of trees.

One would need motorized transportation to make it from one end to another, length *or* depth. One might catch a bus. Take a train.

This was not a mansion—this was a city.

This made a feudal castle look small.

This was Versailles writ large.

He resumed his way up.

From start to finish, it took him a half hour to get up to his duty station.

To the Crow's Nest, that is.

From there, he could look up and *up*—and see the metal steps disappearing into clouds.

This Crow's Nest was a viewing platform that ran around the tower, jutting out about eight feet, with a protective metal railing around it.

A yellow sign with an arrow said: *Seat.*

A sign above this said: *Sit down. Relax. You earned it.*

Yes, he thought. *You made all those steps.*

And you're damned tired.

It felt good to sit down.

He relaxed and took out his duty sheet. Duties 1, 2, 3.

Might as well start with the Outer Bounds. This would be where the border was between Finger property and Rich Man property.

He got a good fix through the hi-tech metal viewer. My, but what fine lens. He adjusted the focus. There they were, the armed cadre walking—and some marching—with their weapons riding their shoulders.

An army squad on patrol.

One armed man had stopped, leaned over, and was lighting a cigarette. Peter zeroed in with his lens. He adjusted for better resolution. Ah!

Perimeter next. He made his way about the Nest, sighting with the viewer lens several men walking and marching. One man dressed in army camouflage stopped and sighted. And then he went back to marching.

Enough of that.

Am I supposed to report men down?

No men down yet.

Rich Man activity next.

Peter went for it.

From a viewer marked Rich Man Eyes scrawled in red marker on masking tape, he could see everything he needed to see. He could even see how some of the Rich Man's mansion disappeared into the tree line. There was mansion back there—in those trees? Yes, that did seem to be the case. But how far did it go? He could glimpse a flash of building—just a glimpse through the sun-lit leafy trees.

High-powered, this thing sure is.

He panned the area with his lens.

Ah, and what's *this*?

A huge truck pulling in. Two men hopping out. Pulling open the rear doors. Another huge truck pulling in.

Both trucks unloading.

More trucks pulling in.

This is *activity*.

Worth noting.

Note it, note it.

He took out his logbook. *Time: 10:37. Activity: Trucks pulling in, unloading.*

He watched. He wrote it all down.

He resumed his viewing through the high-tech viewer.

A man in a charcoal gray suit was now walking about, directing. Then he stopped. The man raised binoculars. He aimed them up at the Crow's Nest. Peter studied the man through the viewer. The man studied him through the binoculars. They studied each other for a good half minute. Then Peter stood away from the viewer. The man put down his binoculars. Peter went back to the viewer. The man raised his binoculars.

This was activity!

He wrote all this down.

The suited man went toward the house.

Peter made his rounds, viewer to viewer: Outer Bounds, Perimeter, Rich Man.

He grew tired of it.

Why hadn't he brought a book?

Next time, a book.

But time went on.

He ate one sack lunch. He drank from his thermos. He finished off a bottle of water.

He made his rounds.

He rested.

He napped.

The day wore on.

He ate his second sack lunch. He drank from his thermos. He finished off a bottle of water.

Once in the night he saw a burst of light, followed by an explosion, and he held his ears. It made a fiery tail and whooshed right by him.

A second one followed.

Then a third.

He lay down and covered his ears and watched as three more shot by him, at closer range.

War zone! He had no helmet. He had no protective gear.

I am a man under attack!

At six the next morning he flicked his flashlight on and began making his way down the winding metal steps, gripping the railing, his backpack loose on his shoulders.

It took him longer than going up. It was scarier going down than going up. He cringed with each step.

When he finally came to the base of the Finger, he noticed a wide entrance—cut into that huge palm of the Finger—leading into a large room flooded with light. He went in. A few dozen men and women were crowded around a table loaded down with food.

"Breakfast time, Professor Boatz!" shouted the woman with the clipboard. "How was your night?"

"How . . . I was shot at. Missiles, or something."

"But you don't look any worse for the wear," said the woman. "Come on, sit down. Eat! Partake!"

She handed him a tray with a plate, silverware, and napkins.

"Thank you."

"Did you do good work?"

"Yes—good."

He heaped his plate up with abundant food.

He sat down.

He dug into a stack of pancakes and fruit, sipped creamed coffee, and pretty soon, the woman with the clipboard rose up at the end of the table. "Now, then, compatriots, finish up. Hurry, hurry! We must move on to battle plans! But dishes first!"

More food remained on his plate.

Why the rush?

Too soon, too soon.

Peter ate quickly.

Several women popped up and volunteered to attend to the dishes. Several men headed outside.

Peter hurriedly ate more and then joined them.

"The thing is," Ernest said, lighting a cigarette, "you hate to spend your *whole* day walking the line, but if you don't, well, that's when they'll attack. Tell me they won't."

"Give them an inch," said another man, flicking his cigarette.

"Give them half an inch," said Ernest. "I don't give a good goddamn if it's a millimeter; Rich Man's bound and determined to bring us down. There you have it."

"Damn straight," said the other man.

A third man laid a hand on both men's shoulders. "Maybe *we* ought to do the attacking. You know that's been *my* argument. Hell, get him before he gets us."

"Not a sound plan," said Ernest.

"You're the expert," said the third man. He turned to the other man. "He's the expert."

"Strategy," said Ernest. "Strategy is all."

"But does it have to be defensive?"

"It's got to be up here," said Ernest, tapping his forehead. "Up here where it counts."

The third man spit. "Well, I know what you mean, but some of us are getting a bit tired of having to *take* it and not giving it back. Know what I mean?"

"Patience," said Ernest, "is a virtue."

The woman with the clipboard yelled from inside. "Meeting— in five."

The men grunted and entered the Finger.

The vast room was busy with tables being scooted together, men and women carrying miniature Fingers, a half dozen men and women working to unroll a huge parchment map onto several long conference tables pushed together.

"Got it," yelled a man, slapping a table.

"Now," said the woman with the clipboard. "Let's all take our seats."

She stood directing traffic as men and women took seats around the map. It was marked with cities, rivers and lakes, mountains, prairies, roads and highways. But what was most prominent were the miniature Fingers spaced roughly equidistant from each other and covering the entire map.

"Reports," said the woman, tapping the clipboard with a pencil.

"Section 1, East," said a woman with long, blond stringy hair. "Funding's up big time! Should be breaking ground by next summer."

"Next summer? Jeez," said the woman with the clipboard. "Couldn't you light a fire? How about spring?"

"I'll put a bee in their bonnet."

"Good for you! East, Section 2?"

"Break ground *today*!"

"Kudos! Kudos!"

A clap-off followed.

"East, Section 3?"

A man fingering a pencil tapped it on the table. "Not going so well. They've raised some earnest money, or something like that. As to putting up a Finger—forget it."

"What's *wrong* with those folks?" said the woman with the clipboard.

"Lack spirit! Drive!"

"Got their priorities confused!" said the woman with stringy hair.

"Yeah, and I'm stuck with them," said the man fingering the pencil. "I'll trade you."

"No, you won't!"

"Fingers Two and Three," piped up one man. "No stopping them folks!"

"They're an inspiration to us all," said the woman with the clipboard. "East, Section 4?"

This went on for a couple hours.

One man stood up. He had a huge gut that swelled his blue Finger tee-shirt. He cleared his throat.

"He's got the floor," said the woman with the clipboard.

"Thanks. That half mile high business? That's good *and* bad. Marketing-wise, good. You *see* it. You can't *help* but see it. Funding-wise, you're talking about a pile of dough, and even if you land ten bucks a pop, that's still a lot of pops."

"True. But we've got to stick to our principles, don't we?"

A white-haired woman stood up. "Listen here, that part's not negotiable. We build them right, or we don't build them at all. *They'll* fork over. Put the fear of god in them, they'll fork over."

A clap-off.

Another white-haired woman stood up. "I second Molly," she said.

"Noted."

A man in a red hunting cap stood up and began banging his deer rifle butt against the table. A few people adjusted their chairs a foot or two away. "Now, you give a *listen* to me. You hear? You give you a good *listen*. This ain't *easy*—it ain't *supposed* to be easy. What I'm a-trying to tell you is this *here*. You take and make them fuckers any less high? You don't get the shit. You don't get the shit, you don't make the point. Every time Rich Man, he shoots off them rockets? Proves his nerves is a-comin' loose." He paused and grinned. "A half mile high? Hell, Finger Three's thinkin' right— a fucking mile high! Hell, make it *five!*" He sat down.

"Whoa!" shouted the woman with the clipboard.

"Had to say my piece," said the man with the deer rifle. "Hope I didn't offend nobody." He looked around. "Didn't, did I? Hope I didn't."

"Naw," said the woman with the clipboard. "We're all grownups, here. Well . . . that concludes this morning's meeting of Command Central, and now—"

"We've got a new man among us!" shouted a man with a bushy beard sitting next to Peter.

"How do we know he's not one of *them*?" shouted out another man.

"He's been vetted," said the woman with the clipboard. "His name is Professor Boatz. He's a welcome addition. He's been on the Crow's Nest. Stand up, Professor."

Peter stood up.

"Thank you," said the woman with the clipboard.

"My pleasure," said Peter.

"And now," said the elderly woman with the clipboard, "as you know, it's time to read from the paper, the key news items that have come to my attention in the past few days. And so . . . let us begin . . . here we have the first one."

"Read 'em up," shouted the man with the red hunting cap. He banged his deer rifle on the table.

"I sure will," said the woman with the clipboard. "I sure will."

She opened a newspaper, rattled it, and read: "Mr. Finger claims he's advancing the cause of humanity. Says Mr. Finger: 'My Fingers are proclaiming to the country, nay, to the entire world, that elaborate wealth is a rip-off of the poor. It is not acceptable. And so, we flip off those who have it. Do I sound angry? I *am* angry.'"

"Fucker ought to be!" shouted the man with the deer rifle.

"*Shush*," said the woman with the clipboard.

"Don't mean to be a problem."

"Don't then."

"No, ma'am, I won't."

The elderly woman with clipboard opened a second newspaper and read: "Rumors abound that certain media persons, radio, TV, and politicians have been taken captive by Mr. Finger's so-called goons. But Mr. Finger responds: 'We always hear such stories when a man sets out to do good. No good deed goes unpunished—isn't that the old saw?'"

She smiled and put this newspaper aside and grabbed up another one. She read: "The Finger Enterprise is changing the country's economy, a recent study has shown. Numerous auxiliary services are needed, and many local towns report a notable improvement in their local economy. Several economists have even made hopeful projections for an increased GDP of five percent or more. 'And this is only a start,' says Mr. Finger. But the newly formed Rich Man's League presents a different picture. Says one spokesman who prefers to remain anonymous: 'We've started siphoning off some of those funds meant to foul the pastoral beauty of this great land.' The Rich Man's League claims that when it comes to pumping up the economy, patriotic citizens will soon 'turn this Finger monstrosity completely around,' seeking the noble instead of the ugly, and when that occurs, the GDP will rise even more."

The woman with the clipboard shook her head, grinned, grimaced, and grabbed up another newspaper. "According to several charitable enterprises, The Finger Enterprise has been shifting the flow of money from the poor and the needy to a cause which amounts to nothing but 'a fascination with the crudest of the crude.'"

The elderly woman banged her clipboard on the table. "Read it and weep, right? So there you have it—in case you missed it in your morning paper." She gazed at them, from one person to another, up and down the tables. "See how we're making the news. See what we're up against? Go and do good work."

Peter was now given Outer Bounds duties, and he strutted with the man with the red hunting cap. A short distance away, more men marched and strutted. Their weapons flashed in the sun.

"We walk the line," said the man. "This here is *the* line, buddy. Or close to it."

"The property line," said Peter.

"Or close to her."

The man stopped, leaned over, removed a pouch from his pocket and began packing a wad under his lower lip.

"But not the actual line," said Peter.

"Safer this way." The man stopped and pointed at the Rich Man's spread.

"I don't doubt it."

"Yeah? Well, I had me an idea. See, I was a-thinkin', just a-thinkin' now, that maybe we ougha sneak in there. Find them rocket launchers."

"Trespassing," said Peter.

The man leaned on his deer rifle. "Seems to me, just thinkin' out loud here, if you had you a good invasion squad, you could sneak over the *actual* line—see that big tree"—he pointed at a large maple tree. "The exact line's about *there*."

"How big a squad?"

"Ten. Most'll probably get caught—them's your breaks, but say one or two gets through, disarms that launcher. Huh?"

"Couldn't Rich Man rearm it?"

"Sure, he could. Probably he *would*."

"So? What's accomplished?"

"You got a point."

He spit a puddle.

"What happens to the one or two who get caught?"

The man with the red hunting cap shook his head. "Wouldn't go good for them fellers. But you takes your chances."

"Bad odds."

"Been fireworks for three straight days. Payback time. Ain't it?"

When it grew dark, and he could hardly walk, Peter limped back to the Finger. The man in the red hunting cap was still marching. He could see his figure in the twilight against a red flame sky.

"I'll need you back on the Crow's Nest tomorrow," said the lady with clipboard.

"Oh, but—"

"Can't you? Please?"

"Yes," said Peter.

He drove out to his motel and collapsed on the bed. When he awoke it was after midnight, and he got up and took a long shower. And then he collapsed again and slept some more.

That Crow's Nest, he thought. Bare bones existence.

Landlubber, aren't you?

The next morning, out at the Finger, several cop cars had pulled up. Three cops were talking to the gray-haired lady with the clipboard. When she spotted Peter, she signaled him forward.

"Tell these officers what you observed the other night," she said.

"Rockets."

"Rockets? What kinds of rockets?"

"Fiery. With long tails."

"Sure they weren't comets?"

"Comets?"

"How many?"

"Ten maybe?"

"Ten," said the officer, writing this down.

The gray-haired lady tapped her clipboard. "We haven't fired any rockets *his* way," she said.

"I wouldn't advise it," said the officer.

"Why is it, then, he can shoot them this way?"

A second officer, a much younger man, stepped forward. "You're the aggressor here, ma'am. He's only responding to the threat you've made."

The first officer laid a hand on the younger officer's shoulder.

"Violence cannot be permitted on either side."

A third officer said to Peter. "Is there a launcher up there, sir?"

"What?"

"Is there a launcher up there—to fire your own rockets?"

"No. No launcher. No rockets."

The third officer turned to the lady with the clipboard. "*Is* there? *Are* there?"

"No, sir, there's no launcher. No rockets."

"Are you sure?"

"Yes, I'm quite sure."

"We'll have a look," said the third officer. "If you don't mind."

"Be careful of the steps."

"What's this? Why did you say that?"

"Narrow," said the woman. "I'm thinking of your safety."

"Oh." The officer headed toward the steps.

The other two officers left. Peter watched them get in their cop cars and drive off.

It took almost two hours, but the officer who went up the Finger came back down wheezing hard. "Drink of water," he cried out. "I need a drink of water!" He leaned against the base of the Finger.

"Step this way," said the gray-haired woman. She led him into the interior of the base. Peter followed her out of curiosity. The map and the miniature Fingers were gone.

Soon, up on the Crow's Nest, he once again monitored Rich Man activity.

Nothing stirring.

He made the rounds, Outer Bounds, Perimeter.

Ah, he had a book this time. He read and read.

It was a thick book.

He ate his sack lunches, drank from his thermos, drank his two bottles of water.

Ah, how pleasant with the book.

It grew dark. He settled back and fell asleep.

He awoke to a bang.

There it *was,* a whoosh of fire with a long tail.

Another!

Another!

Big burst of white light.

An ominous feeling came over him. A sneaking suspicion—he took a dive. Something whammed his head.

He awoke to shaking. "Are you . . . are you *here*? Are you *with* us?"

"What? What?" He started to say Mother, but he knew *that* wasn't right. This wasn't his mother; his mother had gray hair, yes, but this wasn't her. *Who*? And then it came to him: *The Finger. I'm at the Finger.* I'm at the Finger, and this is the woman with the clipboard wanting something. What, though?

"Are you with us, Professor Boatz? Are you with us?"

"Uh . . . yes."

She was rubbing his head. "Listen, now . . . *listen.*"

"Yes?"

"Don't stand up. *Don't stand up* whatever you do."

She wasn't standing up. She was down on her knees.

Up? He looked *up.* Something wrong. Something missing. *Everything* two feet above him. Where was it?

He sat up.

"Don't stand!"

"*No,*" he said, and shuddered.

"Gone," she said, pointing. "It's been sheared right off."

"Oh, my," he said.

"See it down there?" she said.

He turned and looked.

A long column of concrete stretching toward Rich Man's place. Broken.

In many sections.

"We must begin again," said the gray-haired lady. "This is a major setback."

"Yes—major."

"Major."

2

"You want an assignment?" said the lady with the clipboard. "Made for you? Truly for you?"

"Yes, please."

"Logic."

"What?"

"Teach it. You being a professor."

"Yes, I am."

"Go to Finger Two."

"Teach logic?"

"At Finger Two."

"But . . . but . . . logic?"

She whispered at him. *"Yes, Professor . . ."* She gripped his elbow. "They've got a wonderful education program there, I hear—just splendid. And you being a professor." She grinned, whispered. "Captive audience, they've got there."

"Captive—"

"Shush. Your work's done here. You're needed there now. You have much to give." She handed him a map. "That's how to get there."

From the interstate, he could see the towering white monolith fifteen miles off. Finger Two! Even from here, he could detect the distinct features of a human finger.

He soon arrived.

Outside was a great commotion.

Rioters were thrusting up signs: "Down with the Finger," "Screw the Finger," "The Finger Sucks!"

Several armed men stood their ground. One armed man escorted Peter through the mob and into the entrance of Finger Two's huge base—that is, the palm.

An elderly man with a clipboard pulled Peter in, and quickly pushed the door closed behind them. He locked up.

"Such mayhem," said the man.

"I was afraid," said Peter.

"We've been expecting you, Professor Boatz," he said. "Come, and let's talk."

He led Peter into a small lounge area with a coffee pot and snacks. The green tile floor looked freshly waxed.

"What's going on out there?"

"Dissent. But pay no mind. Let's look to our purposes here. Coffee?"

"Yes," said Peter.

The elderly man brought them both coffee.

"Now, I was told about the events at the Finger. Do you know they clipped off a substantial chunk of Finger?"

"Yes."

"That means months and months of fundraising and work, doesn't it?"

"Yes."

"And funds are short. Aren't they?"

"Yes."

"But putting that aside . . . we can use you in the Program. Were you told of the Program? The Education Program?"

"Logic? Teach it?"

The elderly man nodded. Then he said, "What if I were to say, 'Two plus two equals five,' what would you say?"

"You're wrong."

"Why?"

"It's four."

"Why? Let's say I insisted it *was* five, what would you say?"

"You're wrong."

"But what makes me wrong?"

"Because the whole system of math would tumble if—"

"It's analytically true?"

"Yes."

"Good. Let's say we have a syllogism. Let's say it goes something like this: *All men are mortal. Socrates is a man. Socrates is a goat.*

What then?"

"The conclusion doesn't follow from the premises."

"Good. Now, let's imagine this syllogism: All men are goats. Goats like Socrates. Socrates likes men."

"False premises. False ergo."

"Good. Logic is a necessary element of the self-examined life, don't you agree?"

"Yes. But what does logic have to do—"

"With Finger Two?"

"Yes."

"Much."

"It does?"

"Yes. And shall we go for a ride now? Shall we?"

"Of course," said Peter. "But where?"

The elderly man with the clipboard escorted Peter to a door. He inserted a key and turned the doorknob. They came to an elevator.

They entered the car. The exterior side was a large window looking out onto beautiful green rolling hills.

"Rustic, isn't it?" said the elderly man.

"Lovely country," said Peter.

Suddenly rioters burst on the scene, gesticulating with signs: "Fuck the Finger!" "The Finger Sucks!"

"Don't worry," said the elderly man with clipboard. "The glass is unbreakable."

They ascended.

At first the car rode slowly up, but then the elderly man with the clipboard pushed a button and increased the speed.

They were riding fast and high.

And then he pressed the button again. They came to a gradual, easeful stop.

"Note all that," he said.

He panned the world below with a wave of his hand.

Spread out before them on several hills was a monstrously large mansion. It was Rich Man's stately mansion but substantially larger, were that possible.

Was this the Heavenly Abode?

The elderly man raised a finger.

"Most of such spreads, Professor, have doubled and tripled in the last year or two. They require motorized transportation to get from one end of the spread to another."

"I thought as much," said Peter.

"You thought correctly."

He pushed the button again.

The car rose. The elderly man pushed a second button, and the car accelerated. "You know, Professor Boatz, sometimes, when we get this high, I expect to see a face appear at the window. Look— and see if you see what I mean. Just focus on the window itself. Don't look *through* the window. And don't let your eyes drift."

Peter tried not to blink. He couldn't keep from looking *through* the window to the pale blueness that made him dizzy with the ethereal sameness of it all.

"Afraid of heights?" asked the elderly man, eyeing him.

"Somewhat."

"Wait until you get to the Balcony. It's the top of the world."

The car shot up.

It felt like a space launch.

Then the car came to its easeful stop.

The elderly man unlocked the glass window. He slid it open. They stepped out onto a polished white floor with white railing that looked out onto the cloud floor beneath them. "Sometimes," said the elderly man, "I am tempted to take a nice dive over this railing here and fall into that cushiony cloud bed. It would surely hold me up, wouldn't it? At least one might think so."

Peter couldn't take his eyes off of it. One did feel drawn to take a leap.

They ambled about the balcony. This balcony was certainly a much more plush affair than the Crow's Nest at Finger One. Of course he hadn't gone to the very top of Finger One. And now he couldn't since it was blown off. "Was Finger One this nice—at the very top?"

"Finger Two is an upgrade. Mr. Finger has seen reason to improve the product—and the presentation."

They came around a bend. "That—that's—"

"The Nail Room. Mr. Finger's private dwelling place—for rest and relaxation."

Peter put his face up to the window.

"A fine place, isn't it?" said the elderly man.

"It looks . . . plush."

"Yes, quite plush."

Peter had his nose up to the glass, his fingers crawling at it. He wanted to go inside.

"We must go back down now," said the elderly man.

He escorted Peter back to the elevator.

They rode back down.

Or rather plummeted.

They eased to a stop.

"Don't go out *there*," said the elderly man, pointing out the elevator window. Riotous men stormed about with signs. "You'll need an escort, Professor. *Your* world needs to be inside—where it's much more safe, sir. Being a rational man, I'm sure you can fully appreciate that."

He led Peter to a door, unlocked it, and they entered a small room with a twin bed, dresser, and bookshelf stocked with books.

"As you see—your accommodations. Clothes in the dresser. And a shelf of logic books for your perusal. You do know logic, don't you?"

Peter grabbed a book from the shelf: *Logic and Illogic*.

"Yes—"

"Brush up—do. Logic is extremely important, Professor. Logic is the advance guard of the Finger Enterprise. We must defeat ignorance in all its forms. And you, sir, being a professor . . . your skills are much needed here. But it does take a bit of brushup—for you, for me, for everyone in the business."

"I understand."

"Brush up." The elderly man gave the logic books a general wave of his gnarled hand.

"I shall."

"Follow me."

He showed Peter the bathroom, stocked with toilet articles.

"Thanks—"

The elderly man tapped his clipboard. "Well, sir, I must run." He advanced quickly to the door.

It felt so cramped in this place. Peter wanted to go out. He wanted to leave.

"Sir," said Peter. "Sir—"

"Yes? What, Professor?"

"I'll get claustrophobic."

"Claustro . . . well, I'm sorry, sir, but these *are* the accommodations. As cramped as they might seem."

"*Seem?*"

"Think responsibility, Professor," said the elderly man with the clipboard. "Think obligation."

"I will."

Something went off for the elderly man—the proverbial lightbulb. "Let me show you something. Wait here."

Wait here? Where else would he wait?

In a few moments, the elderly man returned.

"Notice in the paper here."

Peter bent over to get a good look.

The elderly man spread the paper out. He began to read: "Reports of captives taken by Finger Enterprises have reached the ears at all governmental levels. Mr. Finger denies these reports and calls them 'vile rumors.' But one official government employee, who prefers to keep his identity unknown, stated: 'Let's understand something. Mr. Finger is an ideologue and zealot and will go to any lengths to advance his agenda. If it were up to me, I would storm each and every Finger with SWAT teams.'"

"Captives," said Peter.

"It's all in a word," said the elderly man with clipboard. "I apprize you of this news item only because you must be prepared for hostility. Ours is to undo—recall what Mr. Twain once said about soap and education."

"I believe it," said Peter.

"We do what we can. And know this: What we do is absolutely

needed to clear up obfuscation of all kinds, rank and vile."

"File?"

"No, vile."

"Oh. Yes, of course."

Peter took a nap.

Three hard knocks on the door. He sat up, confused. Where was he?

He opened the door.

"I tried to awaken you, but you were sleeping the sleep of the dead."

"Yes. I was out."

"This place often has that effect," said the elderly man. "Now, the reason I'm here is that I need you—earlier than expected."

"What time is it?"

"That's not an issue." The elderly man was motioning for him to follow.

They exited the room. The elderly man inserted a key into a lock and turned the doorknob. It was a small conference room with a large blackboard, with yellow chalk smears.

A man in a dark blue suit sat at the end of the conference table. His face was flushed red, and his hands were nervously handling his cup of coffee, like frantic rabbits.

"Coffee?" said the elderly man with the clipboard.

"Sure," said Peter.

"Cream? Sugar?"

"Cream."

"So . . ." said the man in the blue suit. "You've got all the answers. You've got the last word on what's logical, what's sound, verifiable, and what's not."

The elderly man set Peter's coffee cup before him.

"Professor Boatz knows a thing or two about logic, I'm sure," said the elderly man. "I think you will find him quite accommodating. Our student is a TV man," he said to Peter, motioning at the man in the blue suit.

The man in the blue suit sat forward and scooted his coffee

cup an inch ahead of him, and then scooted it to one side. "Here's what I am maintaining," he said. "The *people*, as you call them, don't *want* the Finger. They want what everyone wants, certain basic freedoms. This thing you've constructed here denies them their freedom. That's all I'm saying. How can I possibly be wrong about that? And yet here we are: Session fifteen, twenty—I've lost count."

"I'm well aware of your argument," said the elderly man, "but let's take a moment and list on the blackboard what we have here— you do the honors, sir," he said to Peter.

Peter got up and took a piece of yellow chalk. He felt comfortable with chalk in his hand.

The elderly man nodded at the man in the blue suit. "Proceed, sir."

The man in the blue suit repeated his basic points, and Peter wrote them on the board.

THE PEOPLE DON'T WANT THE FINGER

THEY WANT CERTAIN BASIC FREEDOMS

THE FINGER DENIES THEM THESE FREEDOMS

"What's wrong with that?" said the man in the blue suit. "It's true."

"Well, then," said the elderly man, "let us now examine each of these propositions. The first depends on *who* the people are. Who *are* the people?"

"From what I'm hearing, it's practically everyone but the rich," said the man in the blue suit. He adjusted his necktie.

"Is it?"

"Well, it's at least the people that hate the rich."

"Granted. But what about the second part of the first proposition. It depends on verifiable evidence, does it not? If the people did, in fact, pay for the Finger, this would seem to disallow this first proposition. Would it not?"

"Not necessarily," said the man in the blue suit. "Maybe they paid for something they really don't want."

"So, what you're saying," said the elderly man, "is that they don't know what they want. They shelled out money for something they may not want at all."

"Exactly."

The elderly man turned to Peter.

"But," said Peter, "wouldn't we go more on what their *desired objective* was?"

"Two against one," said the man in the blue suit. "Go ahead, have it your way on the first proposition, but the second, I would think I can find general agreement on."

"Let's consider it," said the elderly man.

"How can you deny that everyone wants certain basic freedoms?" said the man in the blue suit.

"They surely do," said the elderly man.

"But what is the connection between proposition one and two?" asked Peter.

"It's clear to anyone with common sense," said the man in the blue suit. "You're not free if you're doing something that's going to harm you."

The elderly man said, "Let's unpack this. Shall we?"

"If we must," said the man in the blue suit.

"First, how is the Finger harming the people, and how does this harm deny them their freedom?"

The man in the blue suit sat forward. "How is the Finger not harming the people? Hear that disturbance out there! That can't be good for the people, can it?"

"What caused this disturbance?" asked the elderly man.

"What caused it? The people. They caused it."

"And so the people are harming the people."

"Yes."

"Let's knock off for now," said the elderly man, nodding at Peter. "We'll continue this session first thing in the morning."

He nodded at the man in the blue suit.

The man in the blue suit followed the elderly man out of the door. Peter saw the elderly man turn a key in a locked door. He turned the doorknob and pushed the door open. The elderly man waited while the man in the blue suit disappeared inside the room.

"Thank you for your participation," said the elderly man.

"Fuck you!" yelled the man in the blue suit.

The elderly man shut the door and turned the key in the lock. He smirked at Peter. "Some people . . ."

3

Peter's days were long and arduous now, the elderly man appearing at his door to announce breakfast, a breakfast with several other workers in the Cause, in a small cafeteria room—and then, following that, his own conference room. His student population now included the man in the blue suit, another TV guy dressed in a brown suit, a radio talk show host dressed in a tan suit, and a woman radio host in a red suit, and he found it quite difficult to handle four different sets of propositions on the blackboard at any one time, but somehow he managed to do so, and yet he discovered that little ground was gained, as they stuck to their propositions, guarding them jealously, with the exception of a few if they got rattled enough. For facts, the elderly man brought in authoritative sources, but these sources were roundly dismissed as *not* authoritative at all. The elderly man asserted that logic was their only reliable tool. *Truth tests*, he proclaimed: If the correspondence test didn't work, they must at least depend on the coherence.

"You apparently have *your* logic. We have *ours*," said the lady radio host.

"There is but one logical system," said the elderly man. "You can't argue with logic," he assured them.

"But they do," Peter told him in confidence.

"I know they do," said the elderly man, "but keep pounding away."

"But I was told that logic is just my opinion," said Peter.

"That is something we *must* clear up," said the elderly man. "We can't allow that belief to persist."

"But it will, won't it?"

"The ultimate mission of the Finger, sir, is to change minds. We must unmask Untruth for what it is—Untruth."

"And if you do that, which you won't—"

"The Rich Man will fail."

"Which Rich Man?"

"All of them, sir."

"Oh."

"Brush up."

The logic sessions were so heated that Peter found that he needed to take long breaks, and he frequently took naps in his tiny room.

Time was moving on. Soon, he must leave for the university. Back to his regular work.

I've been a worker in the Cause, no? Can't I say I have been, finally, a worker in the Cause?

He brushed up constantly, and he took notes for his conference sessions. He began to like his participants and wanted to help them see the thinking errors they were committing. With slips of papers, he marked his logic books according to types of errors and introduced these principles by careful professorial instruction. But he did confess he had more to learn. He offered to loan his logic books out to his four students, whom he now referred to as seminar members.

"I'm an Icon Man," he said. "Thus, I've got much to learn myself." This he said in order not to humble them too much.

"Are you responsible for *this one*?" asked the lady radio host in the red suit.

"Pardon?"

"Finger Two."

"Oh, no. I didn't contribute a thing. I do tend to be neglectful when it comes to things like that."

"Thank your lucky stars," said the lady radio host.

"Why is that?"

"Because it's not a good thing, and it will come down— probably of its own weight."

"I certainly hope not!" said Peter, recalling the rockets.

4

He had to leave *now*—no further delay. Classes had taken up. He had done his duty.

He was a week late already because of the elderly man's insistence that he stay on—to fulfill his obligations.

He approached the elderly man with the clipboard.

"I *must* leave now," he said.

"But I need you," said the elderly man. "Is it the clientele? I'm sorry, but none of the participants seems to be getting anywhere. I realize that." He shook his head. "Not that you haven't tried. There just seems to be a certain . . . well, obtuseness there. I'm not sure how we get beyond this obtuseness. But I do believe you will break through—eventually."

"Perhaps an ordinary logic course?"

"Instruction is one thing, a closed mind another," said the elderly man. "Yet we must persist. But . . . if you go, sir, I'll have to find a replacement—which is very difficult. The other professorial cadre are growing more busy by the day—with more arrivals. Can't you stay, sir? I beg of you. I do beg of you."

"I really can't," said Peter.

"Well . . . if you must go," said the elderly man, "I will try to understand. I will recommend you to any Education Program you wish."

"The university calls me," said Peter.

"Understood."

The next morning he was on his way out.

He spotted his seminar members filing out of the conference room. They gathered around Peter and the elderly man with the clipboard.

He wanted to wish them goodbye and godspeed.

"You'll hear from the authorities about this," shouted the man in the blue suit. "You can take that to the bank."

"*And* my lawyer," said the woman radio host in the red suit.

"All of our lawyers, and certainly the authorities—*first,*" said the TV guy in the brown suit.

"Why is education so disparaged?" asked the elderly man.

"Show up on my show," said the TV man in the blue suit.

"Or mine," said the man in the brown suit.

"You, sir," said the woman radio host in the red suit. She grabbed Peter's hands. "But I *will* say you do know your logic. No question. And you took such care to make this accessible to us. But, sir, you're not convincing—even so. For all your effort, you lack the right toolkit."

"Toolkit?"

"Do you ever listen to my show?" she asked.

"Uh—no," said Peter.

"There's logic, and there's logic," she said. "You can't reduce everything to book knowledge."

"No?"

"Indeed not. Was the Finger built by logic?"

"Oh, yes," interposed the elderly man with the clipboard. "Yes, indeed, it was! Math, you see, is logic. What if just *anything* went in math—how could we have it? Consider the fine undulations of the Finger, its contours. This involves high-level mathematical calculations. Does it not?"

"Get down," said the man in the blue suit, "to where the real people live. Get your feet planted on the ground, both of you. The rich you hate so much? They've got their feet planted right there— firmly. And this hideous Finger you've constructed? You should build a tribute to them instead. You should celebrate their great accomplishments."

"That's been my message on my show!" said the woman radio host.

"Ah!" said the elderly man with the clipboard. "Let's assemble in the conference room—and discuss this. Shall we?"

"You'll hear from the authorities. And you'll hear from our lawyers."

"I'm afraid we will," said the elderly man when he got Peter off to himself. "Not everyone, you see, appreciates what we do here.

Isn't that sad? I find that very sad."

"It's awful," said Peter. "And after such effort."

"Perhaps some of it *was* appreciated," said the elderly man, tapping his clipboard.

Peter started to go.

"You have a lofty mission," he said.

"Universities don't get out among the people," said the elderly man. "If you ever decide to take on real work, perhaps you'll find your niche at Finger Three. Their Program, I hear, is much more advanced. Much more extensive."

"Thank you," said Peter.

"Logic is the answer, sir. Think of the Greeks."

"Yes . . . but they—"

"No need to discuss. Here."

The elderly man handed him a folded map.

5

"You're a whole week or two late for classes," said the Assistant Dean, "but I've been holding your students for you, thinking that surely you'd return at some point. They, of course, have been *thrilled*. To have that time off, as one might imagine."

He went back to it.

Now and then he listened: for three hard knocks on the door. But they didn't come.

He invited Lucinda Marigold to come over—to give it a second chance.

"I don't know," she said. "I felt your absence. I had no word of your being—here, there, or anywhere. And I'm having a vision problem, you see. I'm trying to make things cohere. I'm looking for a way of understanding roles—yours, mine, ours. I seek a larger frame. Where is this larger frame?"

And so he went back to living alone.

He went back to his research, his writing, and his classes.

Mercy Merry met him at the Faculty Club. "Two men in suits were looking for you. They looked unequivocally official."

"Two men?"

"What have you done?"

He grew grim. Of course, of course.

"Is it something serious?"

"Yes," he said. "Quite serious." He mentioned authorities, attorneys.

"What?"

"Logic," he said. "It had to do with that."

"I don't accept logic," she said. "It's patriarchal, masculine, and it assumes principles that remain yet to be proved."

"Axiomatic," he said.

"You'd better watch out," she said. "Apparently you've ruffled some feathers."

He asked her to teach his classes.

At night he waited for the three hard knocks on the door. Why didn't they come? If they were asking about him, why didn't they?

"Probably," said Mercy Merry, "because they want you to sweat it out. You can stay with me."

"But I'm your professor," he said.

"Have you forgotten?"

He admitted he hadn't. "But should we up it?" he asked.

"Why *not* up it?"

"Well."

"Oh, don't be so old fashioned. Besides, who cares? Do you care? Do I care?"

"No," he said.

"You will give me an A regardless, isn't this true?" she said.

"How can I not?"

"And the classes," she said. "No public appearance. You must resign yourself to that fact."

"Hide out?"

"Yes."

"But what about the classes? The grades?"

"Leave that up to me."

He moved in. She said she didn't mind if he slept with her. And sex was okay too, just as long as he didn't sexualize, or rather *genderize*, it in any way. "You know what I mean, don't you?" she said.

"Yes. I do."

"Don't think of yourself as *the man*, me as *the woman*."

"I won't," he said, yet the latent athlete in him sprang forth—he couldn't help but take the predatory initiative.

"And don't worry about results," she said. "I've had my tubes tied."

"What? Already?"

"Yes, indeed. Done and done."

Meanwhile, he asked the Assistant Dean about the authorities. Did she know anything? Had any suited figures asked about him—wearing black, perhaps?

"Not that I know," she said. "What's up?"

He told her of his logic lessons: of his captive audience at Finger Two, of the failure of the logic principles to take hold, of the outrage on the part of the man in the blue suit, et al.

"Sounds to me," said the Assistant Dean, "as though you need to be on the lam—until this thing blows over."

"Good advice," he said.

"I *can* be a friend," said the Assistant Dean. "In case you haven't noticed."

"The book," he said, attempting to skirt.

"Yes?"

"I knew nothing, nothing. I knew absolutely *nothing* about it—about the Finger."

"What's to know? What didn't you know?"

"Everything."

"Be specific. I hate clouds, Peter."

"You do?"

"Please."

"I wasn't in the trenches before, but then I *was*. It's different in the trenches."

"I could have told you that. But would you have listened? It's crude, so crude, isn't it? Therefore, poetry—you see. That's why the poetry, Peter. And the idiot didn't even read it!"

"I know."

"But what? I hear a *but*, Peter."

"I had hoped for transcendence, but I was . . . I was mired down."

"You were in the news, but then that's not transcendence, is it?"

"No."

"*Is* there transcendence in the Finger, Peter?"

"Is there transcendence period?"

"Yes, Peter, there is. Do not doubt it. Please do not."

"Perhaps if you can escape the creeping of a soiled humanity on your soul—I do not like to be mired in the dross, Lucinda."

"Oh, Peter—"

"Yes—"

"I love to hear you call me my name. I do."

He suddenly felt great affection for her.

"But then you dump me," she snarled. "For less. For cheaper fare—*she* appeared to be dross, Peter."

Sheila, of course.

Obvious malice from a woman who perceived herself dumped.

And was *being* dumped, in point of fact.

For . . . Mercy Merry.

Though, of course, the Assistant Dean knew nothing of that. Ah . . .

He informed Mercy Merry of his revised thinking: that hiding out here, in these environs, wasn't enough. No, indeed not. "I must, in point of fact, hightail it *out* of here," he said.

She insisted on going with him.

"Why?"

"Because."

"Because why?"

"Because I want an *adventure*. I'm tired of *not* having an adventure. I'm tired of books, books, books, written by idiots who don't know the first thing about life."

This hurt. He thought of his own book.

"Which is?" he asked.

"Which is *what*?"

"The first thing about life."

"What do they know about blood, saliva, thirst and quenching that thirst, hunger and food, surfeit, about energy and lethargy, about inspiration and ennui?"

"They know a lot!" he objected. "At least some of them do."

"Name one."

"Me. My book," he said.

"I haven't read that."

He grabbed up a copy of his manuscript—from a cardboard box. He was living out of suitcases and boxes.

"Read that," he said.

"Quite a tome," she said, flipping pages.

"A good tome," he said.

Yes, indeed, he stood by it. Perhaps the world wasn't up to it, but he must stand by it.

The Assistant Dean was correct on that score.

"And if I do, what mind-forged manacles? What linguistic treachery?"

"None!"

"Well, then." She continued flipping pages. "One, I'll read it. Two, I'm going."

"But who'll teach the classes?"

"Joyce Early."

At first he was shocked. But then he said, "Good choice. Solid."

"She's a nitwit," said Mercy Merry, "but what difference does it make? She's sort of the devil's advocate, don't you think?"

"Seems to me."

"When do we leave?"

He thought of the three hard knocks.

"Right now. This very minute."

"My car, then," she said. "They'll never suspect that."

"Off to Finger Three."

"Finger what?"

"Three. And *there's* an adventure for you," said Peter.

And yet he really did not want to be in the Program, advanced or not. But what options?

"Where's your proof?"

"I have none."

"Okay," she said. "Let me pack."

"And me as well," he said.

They loaded the car with cardboard boxes, luggage, and trivial amenities, and left.

"Travel light," she said. "It's always best to travel light."

"I feel that way too," he said. But was he? With two suitcases and seven cardboard boxes?

6

Peter drove. They drove all night. Mercy Merry said she liked driving straight—no stops. Road trips felt to her like the flow of electricity, and did one wish to pull the plug? No, one did not. Make them fast and furious, and risk exceeding the speed limit. In fact, *do* exceed it every opportunity. On the interstate, the drivers determine the speed, she said. Cops have to suck it up. Wasn't that correct? Didn't he think so?

"I never thought of it that way," said Peter. "But yes, I think you're right."

"Then exceed the speed limit," she said.

Her foot went for his foot.

"Okay!"

She removed her foot.

He pressed down on the accelerator.

She had slept all night, but now she was reading his book. He heard pages turning.

Pages rubbed between fingers, turning, rubbed.

Turning.

Paper sounds. Who didn't like paper sounds? Such materiality, and yet could his book be limited by paper? No. *There is so much beyond the paper*, he wanted to cry out. Dig deep!

He hoped she would.

Now and then he looked.

How fast. Her eyes all over the page.

A brilliant woman, brilliant.

An hour went by.

"I'm so thirsty," she said.

It was heartfelt.

"We can stop."

"So hungry."

"We can stop."

He pulled over the first chance he got. He hurriedly got her two bottles of water. What if some criminal kidnapped her, sitting out there in that car alone? You heard of such things. "What to eat?" he asked.

"Drive on."

He drove on.

Another hour went by.

She read and read.

The woman was devouring that book.

There was something there, surely.

Something lifting her up, up, up!

But he worried.

"Won't you get sick reading like that?" he asked.

She gulped water.

"Um."

"Won't you?"

"No."

"We could stop someplace. So you could finish."

"No. Keep driving." She motioned at his foot. "Pedal it down, Professor."

"Oh, sorry," he said. He pushed down on the accelerator.

Up to eighty now.

His cell phone went off.

"Your cell," she noted.

"Yes. I know this."

He reached for it, inside his pocket.

The screen: *Sheila calling.*

No, no.

"Aren't you going to answer it?"

"No."

"Okay. But it's grating...grating...it's somewhat exasperating."

It stopped, of course.

She kept reading.

Another hour went by.

"You're almost done," he observed.

"Yes."

"You've pretty well read through the book!"

"Um," she said.

"I like that," he said. "That's fine, fine, and I like it."

"I'm getting so tired," she said. "We'll have to stop—for a motel."

"I thought you didn't like stopping."

"I don't—but I'm tired. And besides, we must make time for sex. So we'll stop off at a motel soon—not at night, like your average person so *ordinarily* does. We'll stop off in bright daylight and have sex that way. What do you say?"

How could he say he wasn't game? Why wouldn't he be?

"Pull off . . . in say thirty minutes," she said.

"Sure. Because by then you'll be done with the book?"

"Um."

Well, this was a bright spot. Done with the book—and sex to follow.

Bright, very bright.

In the motel, just as they were getting undressed, his cell went off.

"Your cell."

"I know."

"Who *is* it?"

"No one."

He glanced at it. Yes, *her*. It was *her* all right.

"I don't get it," she said. "Why don't you answer your cell?"

"I don't want to," he said. "I don't want to answer it."

"Come to me," she said.

Afterwards, she spoke of his book. "Grand narrative," she said. "I knew it, just knew it—as soon as you mentioned it. But you're right, there's more. I was so *thirsty*—and I am again. Just speaking of it . . . I am *again*."

She leaped out of bed and flashed for the bathroom. "I'm feeling it *again* . . . oh, ever so much!"

The water ran hard.

"*Oh*," he cried. Thirst—he did like that. Thirst for *more*, oh how divine!

"Tremendously!"

She came back with a full glass.

"Water," he said.

She drank it down fast.

She looked at him, closely, as though she were about to impart a long-held secret.

She moved toward him. Would she take him again, in her lovely arms?

"Professor Boatz, my love . . ."

"Yes?"

"My dear Professor, just thinking of it. Imagining it . . . I'm seeing it now, *again*, how that poor sap was locked away inside a brick wall to die of hunger and thirst! The desert drought in his mouth—I was just parched to think of it."

"But hunger too, you said . . ."

After all, *two* senses, not one.

"No—it's been thirst, mostly. And why question it?"

She hurried back—into the bathroom. The water ran hard.

She came back out—with another full glass.

"An unusual reaction," he said. "I had no idea."

She drank down the glass. Almost in one gulp.

And then she fixed her eyes on him. "Which is next—food or second sex?"

He tried to choose. They were both so good. "I would say . . ."

"I want something to eat first," she said. "Okay?"

"Sure."

"How can we decide?" she said, "between food and second sex? Is there an actual criterion?"

He shook his head. "It's in the gut, mainly."

"Yes, of course—we humans are creature of our moods . . . one must be frank."

But this disturbed him: what *he'd* said—and what *she'd* said.

He grabbed her hand, restrained her from springing for the doorknob. This woman was on a mission for that motel restaurant.

But he had a beef.

"First," he said. "First, my dearest—"

195

"Yes, darling?"

"Speaking of that one criterion—that one criterion business?"

"There is none."

"But—"

"No buts."

So bent on that doorknob, this woman was.

"You *do* appear to be right."

"Oh, good," she said, and brightened. And softened.

Yet he continued to grip her hand, to restrain, to hold her back—just in case.

The point must be dealt with first, the food second.

"A point of discussion," he said.

"Yes, Professor."

"As I've just conceded," Peter said, "one standard, or criterion, governing choice *is* indeed problematic."

"It's utterly indefensible."

"Well, at least in some cases."

"In *all.*"

"That's yet to be decided. But an example in your favor: For instance, let us assume you're situated betwixt two elevators, one on each side of the hallway, equally distant. Now, then, what criterion tells you that Elevator A is a better choice than Elevator B?"

"Exactly," said Mercy Merry.

"Even so, this may be but an isolated example."

She smiled with an air of tolerance. "It's all animal need, Professor."

"Flesh, not spirit?"

"Perhaps both."

"Agreed," said Peter.

"But we'll never know."

"But—"

"I tire of this," she said. "Food—I want food."

I could have asked for a definition of both.

But he was hungry too.

They landed in on the motel restaurant, and she ate huge helpings. She drank no end of water.

"Unusual." he said.

"You're still on the water," she said.

"Yes."

"Your book worked, Professor, on my very *soul*. Do you want to challenge that?"

"No."

"And now it's time for more love," she said. "Second sex."

How could he argue?

"You aren't going back to—"

"No," he said.

"Good."

Afterwards, she wanted to set the alarm for two.

"Two?"

"I love driving in the dark," she said. "Don't you?"

"I *did* drive in the dark," he said.

"So far."

"I love riding in the dark," he said.

"Then this plan will work out wonderfully."

At two, they tried to get up, but couldn't.

At three, they stumbled out of the motel and got back in the car.

Mercy Merry took the wheel.

They were soon back on the interstate.

He dozed off.

He awoke to her shaking him. "Professor Boatz," she said. "Stay awake. I'm getting sleepy—*so* sleepy."

He saw the speed. Ninety.

"*I'll* drive," he said. "Please, *me*."

"Okay . . . because I *am* about to fall asleep. I think maybe I *was* asleep."

"Oh, no," he said. "No, no. *I'll* drive."

She pulled over.

It was a welcome relief.

He got behind the wheel. He got back on the road.

"I need some *coffee* myself," he said. "Sugar, or *something*—"

She nestled up to him. "You're *my* sugar, Professor Boatz."

Tears sprang to his eyes.

"I'm glad, so glad," he said, gripping her hand.

And then, it struck him. He had not questioned that appellation at all, perhaps due to the cloud of sex, but now perhaps he should.

"But please . . . please don't call me Professor Boatz. I'm not your professor anymore."

"Just because you slept with me? How *was* it, by the way?"

"Splendid. Couldn't have been better."

"Students typically sleep with their professors."

"Uh—typically?"

"Perhaps I've overstated it. It's not untypical for students to sleep with their professors."

"It's against university ethics."

"Are we at the university?"

"No."

"Where *are* we?"

"In your car, heading for Finger Three."

"In my car. Where's your proof?"

This. He touched the dashboard. He slapped the steering wheel.

"And what is the ontological status of *this*?"

Someone—was it *him*?—had taught her too well.

"Ontological status?"

"First off, what's *your* mean? And second, how is it that anyone could be *in* a car? What is the psychological, existential, social, political, or linguistic status I am to infer from the referents *your* and *in*? Who are the stakeholders? What are the stakes?"

"You're still my student," he said.

"No, you're *my* student."

"How so?"

"We are each other's students."

It sounded like a good argument to him.

They could see Finger Three a good thirty miles off in the early morning sun.

It glinted off the top in a red haze through a gray coil of cloud cover.

"I think I see the Nail," said Peter.

"Nail?"

"As in *finger*nail."

"You can't see the Nail," she said.

"Yes, I do think I can see the Nail. Look ... way up. Up, up. The cloud cover obscures it a little."

"A lot."

"But you can still see it."

"No. I don't see it."

When they finally came to it and parked the car, two men in Finger Three tee-shirts with Finger Three ball caps guided them into paved parking spaces.

Paved.

A welcome upgrade indeed.

They wanted to know the nature of their visit.

"To teach," said Peter.

"Teach? Teach what?"

"Logic."

"Ah—yes. Well, then," said one man, adjusting his ball cap. He had a wide space between his upper front teeth. "In the *Program*?"

"Yes."

"Your credentials, sir?"

Peter told him. He told him about Finger Two.

"I am Professor Boatz," he said.

"Ah, Finger Two."

"I want a more advanced Program," Peter said.

"More advanced? Well this is certainly more advanced." The man looked at Mercy Merry. Was that a leer?

She picked up on it. "I am his paramour," she said. "Every sexual act he requires, I willingly perform. Do you have any problems with that?"

"Not me," said the man with the gap between his teeth. "Do you teach too?"

"Yes, I do teach, when I am not otherwise occupied."

"What do you teach?"

"We teach logic," said Peter. "Both of us."

Mercy Merry shook her head. "No. I do *not* teach logic. I teach the way logic is predicated on false premises."

"Go with your gut?"

"No, indeed not. Well, sometimes. But I do not accept any statement as true. No statements. In fact, I loathe statements."

"That will do, I suppose," said the man with the gap. "Most of us have tired of statements. We deal with such a rash of them. Your credentials?"

"We have credentials," said Mercy Merry. "Though I do not accept a one of them."

The man with the gap in his uppers sighed. "We can try you out. I can't guarantee anything."

"*Who* can guarantee anything? Tell me what *guarantee* means, anyway."

"Precisely," said the man with the gap. "Please. Follow me."

7

Peter grew used to life at Finger Three. When he thought back to Finger One, he thought: *primitive.* Finger Two: *limited.* But Finger Three? Such bountiful options. A spacious library, well stocked, with comfortable couches for reading; a recreation room with Ping-Pong and badminton tables, an indoor swimming pool. And decidedly comfortable living accommodations.

His king-size bed with Mercy Merry.

"I want a waterbed," she said.

"Just request it," said Peter.

One was installed.

"Ah!" she cried. "Now this is putting on the Ritz!" She rolled around on it.

Mercy Merry, he thought. Happy, happy, happy.

Except now and then she'd say, "I could get bored here. I could."

"Don't say that," he said. "Please don't."

"Why not? It's true."

"It's not an adventure?"

"What's an adventure?"

"True," he said.

But for him, it was.

And best of all, the elevator.

The car ride at Finger Three had more complex features: varied speeds, piped-in music of one's own choice, visions of the outside like Finger Two but which could be refracted in surprising ways by the mere push of a button. And the Rich Man Three Viewing Station: such elegance, the fine white marble parapet, and such a magnificent view of RMT's mansion laid out on thirty hills. But one couldn't be certain, Peter thought, about this matter of beauty— that is, its ontological status. Where *was* the beauty? Was it in the *view* from Finger Three, or was it in the mansion *itself*? He puzzled over this conundrum to no end.

The heights, as the car rocketed up, gave him such a feeling of lightness. He swooned. He swallowed several pills, feeling an inordinate compulsion to take an easeful swan dive into the depths below. A daily airy swim. It seemed so right.

Mercy Merry with that flaming red hair suddenly perked up and claimed she had fallen in love with him, her professor. "*You* are my adventure, dearest," she enthused.

"Me?"

"Women do that, you know? They fall in love with their professors."

"Of course," he said.

"I devoutly love you. Sex has never been better. Time with you has been . . . is . . . so utterly divine."

"Uh . . . well," he said.

This somehow disturbed him.

This schmaltzy stuff.

Where was the true Mercy Merry?

"I object," he said, "on several counts. For one, I'm not, as I've pointed out, your professor."

"We've been over it. I tire of the discussion," she said.

"But perhaps I *am* your professor," he said.

"Actually, I've romanticized all this," she said. "But we all need our myths. They don't mean a thing, of course, but we do need them in spite of this."

"But does this mean that you don't love me?"

"What's love?"

"Affection? Caring?"

"Where is this lodged? Does it spill out so we can measure it?"

"What if we *could* measure it?" asked Peter.

"You want the truth?"

"About what?"

"About you, about me, about love."

"I don't know. I'm not sure. No, I don't think so."

"You're a better lover than professor, Professor Boatz."

"Really?"

She let this soak in.

He recoiled at it.

"Was I so bad in the classroom? I *was* good, wasn't I?"

"You *are* good, but how can the classroom ever measure up to this?"

He thought she was right about that. Certainly, it couldn't.

They became co-teachers in the Program of Rigor.

The Program Head assembled them together in a large, spacious office.

An orientation, he said. It was in order.

He was a short man whose large desk stacked high with papers seemed to swamp him. He tended to dice each thought up before delivering it, as though words needed to come in bite-size pieces before his listeners could swallow them.

"Logic," he said, "is . . . you must understand . . . at the heart of the Finger. At least of Finger Three . . . I can speak only what I know of, you see."

"Experience," said Mercy Merry.

"Mental," said the Head.

"Which *is* experience surely as much as the physical."

"Mental," said the Head. "Think of logic as the base itself . . . as the foundation of all social reform . . . and improvement. Think of the Enlightenment itself . . . think of reason. Reason, my dear compatriots in the Cause."

"Yes, reason," said Peter. "It must reach true heights—if it can. If it really can."

"It can," said the Head.

"Un-reason," said Mercy Merry. "I prefer un-reason."

"Certainly not. It's what we fight . . . we mount a brave war against un-reason," said the Head.

"As you wish," said Mercy Merry.

"I do . . . wish. You've ridden the car . . . up?"

"Yes, oh, yes," said Peter. "Many times. In fact—"

"Logic," said the Head.

"Ah!" said Peter.

"The Law of non-contradiction. Fundamental, isn't it . . . to the building of this and the other Fingers . . . fundamental to the Program . . . and yet consider . . . how the destroyers have . . . they've always, you see, worked for its perversion. Reason and logic, my dear compatriots, my fellow strugglers in the Cause. We aim high here . . . as high as the Finger itself."

"I see," said Peter.

"I don't," said Mercy Merry.

"Logic is the beauty . . . the essence . . . perhaps you see only the Finger, flipping off the Rich Man? Perhaps that's all you see?"

"No," said Peter. "No."

"It doesn't bother you?"

"A little," said Peter.

"Think on it," said the Head, and rose. He shook both of their hands.

"Glad to be shut of him," said Mercy Merry.

"A deliberative man," said Peter. "I believe he knows the essence."

"A zealot," said Mercy Merry. "I hate each and every one of them."

He did think on it. How logic somehow purified Finger Three flipping off Rich Man Three from as much as thirty miles away, a clear and visible destination point on the interstate. My, my, now *that* was a distance.

Logic, the fine books on the shelves.

The Program of Rigor.

So nicely structured:

First, the morning meeting with the plenipotentiary speaker.

Then break-out sessions in conference rooms.

Then the wrap-up with P.S.

"We were designed to co-teach," said Mercy Merry. "Weren't we now?"

Designed? By whom? Or what? He didn't take it up.

But he had to admit, he'd always co-taught with Mercy Merry.

Remembering back, he saw that red flame lighting a fire and spreading from one seminar member to another. Who could defeat this woman's logic, or, as she contended, her non-logic?

Usually the break-out sessions were filled with an assortment of TV hosts, radio hosts, politicians, a few movie stars, and even a few rich men. Peter growled that sessions went nowhere.

"Where do you expect them to go?" asked Mercy Merry.

"In a logical direction!" He regretted these words as soon as they were out of his mouth.

And yet she didn't attack him on this quarter. "What they need, I think, is a new vision. I'm thinking: 'Take them up the elevator. Give them a ride.'"

This sounded ominous. But he agreed.

They invited a politician with a burgundy tie.

"Sure," he said. "You don't have to twist my arm. And even if you did, I'm used to your twisted logic."

Peter decided not to take offense. If one did one's best, what else could one do?

The three of them rode the car up. And Peter meanwhile demonstrated the car's decidedly impressive special options. "Note," he said, "the music."

A flood of Wagner filled the car. He switched to Chopin. And then to Beethoven.

"That's very nice," said the politician. "Though is this anything new? We've come to expect elevator music, haven't we?"

"But we control it ourselves," Peter pointed out.

"What we expect shapes our response," said Mercy Merry.

"I guess that's right," said the politician.

"Now," said Peter, "watch this." He varied the speed, accelerating, then slowing, and then shooting up like a bottle rocket, and then gradually slowing to a stop at the RMT Viewing Station.

They remained in the elevator car.

"Goddamn," said the politician. "You trying to kill me?"

"You didn't enjoy that?"

"I'm not a kid, you know. Maybe a kid would enjoy such erratic disturbances, but I'm a grown man."

"Well, I do apologize," said Peter. "But take a look."

They looked out on the thirty hills where Rich Man Three's vast holdings lay. There was a to-scale model down below under glass, but this was the *real* thing. Such pristine land, richly green as the darkest spinach, lovely trees in a splendid array of innumerable geometric shapes, and swimming pools—there were at least a dozen of them. Ah, and a fleet of automobiles of the finest manufacture, with gleaming finishes—dark blue, gray, black, maroon—assembled in some sort of formation, perhaps for gaudy display? So much like heaven this all was, so . . . nice and fine and . . . unearthly . . . earthy but unearthly too. Perhaps it was the bright sun on the spinach-colored grass, or was it the bright sun winking through the white wisps of cloud floating ever so easefully over the one hundred-acre rambling mansion? Yes, it *was* one hundred acres, according to that to-scale model housed in the glass case in Finger Three's spacious atrium. And such interminable bright red mansion brick—matching the bright red winding drives and walkways—perhaps a foretaste of heavenly mansions, driveways, and walkways?

"What pig owns all that?" sneered Mercy Merry.

"But it's so . . . breathtaking," said Peter.

"Now, that *is* nice," said the politician. "Very nice, isn't it?"

Peter used the refraction choice. "Consider this," he said.

The view shifted gradually so that it was more obliquely represented. The mansion bowed out, grew fatter.

"That's even more interesting," said the politician. "But I don't think it's quite accurate."

"How so?" asked Mercy Merry.

"You think I want to answer *you*?" said the politician. "It's like a funhouse mirror. Is that accurate?" He gave Mercy Merry a quick scowl.

"It's as accurate as any—"

"Shut the fuck up," he said to Mercy Merry. "I know you're my professor, but really, would you just shut up?"

"All right. You certainly have the option of demanding this."

"I do. I know. And I'm exercising it."

"Let's go to the Top," said Peter. "Are you ready?"

"I would love to see the very top," said the politician. "I would love to do anything but those godawful seminars."

"You should appreciate them, for they are given from the heart and mind," said Mercy Merry.

What an odd thing to say.

But he loved her for it.

"I thought I told you to shut up," said the politician.

"Is this how you treat all women?"

"Please, just let me *be*," said the politician. "So I can enjoy."

The elevator was careening up.

All the way.

When they stepped out, Peter could tell. There was something different today—in the air, in the atmosphere, in the cloud cover.

It was suffused and soaked with scintillating sun.

All three of them started to mount the Top's white marble railing. They each held the other's hand and gripped tightly.

The politician came down first.

"I would have gone over," he said, "if it hadn't been for you. Oh, thank you—thank you to my dying day."

"I felt the pull myself," said Mercy Merry.

Peter continued to hold her hand. "What have we learned here?" he asked.

The politician grunted. "I don't know a goddamned thing we've learned. Well, correction: Me, I want to stay on solid ground. You want to come up here yourself, you go ahead."

"Okay," said Peter.

The politician pointed a finger at the two of them. "You do read the papers, don't you?"

"Yes," said Peter. They had numerous papers down in the recreation lounge. He enjoyed keeping up with the news—principally about the Finger. It was scaling up, and up, in the GDP. One economist called it a major contender. Another said it would crumble, most likely, especially with the new *umph* the Rich Man's League was getting. Money was coming in from all quarters, oddly enough. "Yes, I read it all the time," said Peter. "Because so much is happening these days."

"Hear me, then," said the politician. "Hear me well. They're coming for you—you and your kind. Maybe they haven't come yet, but they're coming, and there will be a day of reckoning."

"Reckoning of what?" said Mercy Merry.

"I'm *not* talking to you," said the politician.

"He doesn't like heights," Peter told her later.

"Oh, he likes them all right," said Mercy Merry. "He was the one that was going to leap off. He about took the two of us with him!"

8

"It seems to me," said Mercy Merry, "that we've about run our course."

"How do you figure?"

They'd been there months on end, she said.

Or was it years.

"Six months," said Peter. "That's all."

"Time is what you *experience*," said Mercy Merry. "The rest is nonsense. I've had my adventure. It's time to go."

"I'm still on the lam," he said.

"I'm not."

"You will be."

"Oh," she said.

He was in the middle of a conference session when his cell phone went off.

"You confiscated ours," said the politician with the burgundy tie.

"Cell phones are not recommended," said Peter.

"And so there's yours, and it goes off?"

"Point well taken. Give me just a minute."

He dared not open the door. They might make a rush for it.

Of course where would they get off to?

Still, it would end the session, and he had so much to accomplish.

Sheila's number flashed on his screen.

Why, *why*?

Did he dare?

He looked about, at three radio hosts, two TV hosts, and four politicians.

They looked grimly at him.

"Who is it? Your girlfriend?" sneered a politician in a black suit.

"Old one," said Peter, and quickly punched the right key. And then he said, "Hello, Sheila."

"Oh, Peter, Peter, *Peter*, please, don't leave me holding like this. I . . . do you know that I have . . . ever since you left, been waiting, waiting for a word. From you—a word from you. But do you think I would call? No, because it was *your* job to do the calling—"

"You did call," said Peter. "Twice."

A silence.

Ghostly.

"And you didn't answer."

"No—I was . . ."

"No excuses, please. But now, having waited until I can wait no longer, here I am, before you, your woman. Your lover. Your Sheila."

"Put it on speaker phone!" shouted out a radio host. "So we can all hear."

Peter shook his head.

"I can't talk right now," he said.

"You *will* talk right now," said Sheila. "I can wait no longer, Peter. I have waited for you my entire life. At least, my entire *sexual* life. And now you must decide."

"I did decide."

"Decide again, Peter. How can you turn away your delightful Sheila? Your loving, scintillating Sheila? Don't you remember the Compendium? Don't you remember any of it?"

"Yes."

"I will give you no more, Peter—no more than another three days to decide. And that's it. And then it's Plan Two."

"I thought you already *exercised* Plan Two."

"Three, then. If you must be so literal about it."

"Oh, well, I must, I absolutely must . . . go."

"Don't you recall sex with your pretty Sheila, Peter? How good it was?"

"Yes—"

"And don't you want babies with your dear Sheila?"

He looked about at the men and women dressed nicely in suits, but all of them hating him. Why should men and women in suits hate him when he was simply trying to teach them logic? Trying to assist them in that noble pursuit of pure reason, the key mission of Finger Three?

"I'm not sure about babies," he said.

"Okay. Well, then no sex. And no Sheila."

"I guess not."

"Three days, Peter. And then I'm coming for you. You will not be able to resist me because I know you. You love the *flesh*, Peter, and if you know anything about me, I *am* the flesh, darling."

Yes, he thought, she *was* the flesh.

She was an abundance of the flesh.

But then so was Mercy Merry.

"I know," he said. "I never doubted it."

"This world," she said. "Forget the one dancing in your head. Please, Peter, before it's too late."

"Too late for what?" he asked.

"Did you get nothing at all out of the Compendium?"

"Sure," he said. "But I've got to go."

"Three days."

He had been longing for the Nail Room—the special observatory room at the Top, encircled by the white marble railing—but that was a privilege, he was told, of the higher-ups. He, they advised him, was rather low on the totem pole. At Finger Two, it was Mr. Finger. Here it was the higher-ups, whoever they were.

Bureaucracy, of a mystifying kind.

"Status," he said. "I guess we don't have it."

"We can't have everything we want," Mercy Merry said.

But he longed terribly for it. He wanted the heights, and he wanted it more permanently. The elevator ride had served to whet his appetite—he was ravenously hungry for more.

"Why can't we?" he said.

"Bribe someone."

"No," he said. Besides he had no money. And he couldn't risk using a card.

"Well, I guess *I* could."

"What?" And then he got her drift. "No," he said.

"A hint works better than an act," she said. "Think about it."

"You wouldn't, though."

"Never."

Could he trust her? Could he?

It didn't take long.

They soon gained entrance.

And then, then, could he trust her since they *had* actually gained entrance to the Nail Room, with its elegant furnishings, its full bar, its satellite TV? Its piped-in music controlled by the mere push of a button? Could he?

And then, *then*, could he when their entrance to that room became more frequent? Could he?

"*Did* you?"

"No—I guarantee, I did not do it."

"Please," he said. "I hope you didn't. If you did, level with me. Did you?"

"I did not do it." she said. "I did not. And I never will. I only hinted."

"But that counts as a promise of a kind, doesn't it?"

"No. Because what *is* a promise?"

"I *know, I know*," he said, knowing her answer already to that one. They'd discussed it before. Even if you signed your name on a document, what was that signature but a signature? And if you considered it further, what was the ink but ink? "It's what it suggests," he'd said. And she'd shot back: "Lots of things suggest lots of things." And he'd said, "What about *legal* documents?" And she'd shot back: "Why, my professor, does a signature make *anything* legal?"

"Because we agree that it does. It's a covenant of a kind."

"What's agreement worth?"

"Everything."

"What if we agree to kill each other?" asked Mercy Merry.

"Illegal."

"Why?"

There was no solving it.

And now this Nail Room.

Gained by covenant?

"At some point," she said, "we won't be able to use it—when they realize they've been had."

"They? There's more than one?"

"A figure of expression."

"Then there's only one," he insisted.

"Yes."

"You will guarantee me that?"

"Yes."

He felt better. He breathed better.

The settling in had been—well, so wonderfully nice. To reflect on, that is, to rehearse in his mind. Moving from their accommodations down below, moving up, up, up to this fine, fine Nail Room—at first with only a few articles of clothing, some toilet articles, a book or two—and the two of them prepared then for only a *short* stay . . . but now—yes, now, he was *claiming* the place. She was claiming it. And what *was* claiming? Why it was a key principle of happiness theory, that's what it was.

Ours now. *Ours.*

I'm happy!

You're happy!

We're happy!

A workman in blue wheeling in his many boxes, their suitcases, on a dolly.

Back and forth, back and forth.

Over there, yes—pile them in that closet there. Yes, that's right.

And then, all concluded, workman now gone. The two of them—alone now.

Matching Greek Revival bed and sofas. He ran his hands over these fine specimens.

"You like it all so much," she said. "Don't you?"

"Greek Revival."

"And so?"

"It's ours."

"And so?"

"What?"

"What does it all suggest—to you?"

"It's so . . . elegant," he said.

"But what does it all suggest?"

"I don't know. Let me work on that."

He chose Mozart. Piped in, and full-bodied, filling the air, resonating in his very pores. Ah, Mozart.

"Shall we tip one?" he asked, as she migrated to the bar, for the second—no, it was the third time.

"Oh, we shall," she said. "But you must make your own."

"Yes, and I will make yours too," he said.

"No, you will not."

"Oh," he said.

"I do not mean to be snarky," she said.

He let it go.

With drinks in hand, they lounged in the Greek Revival bed, their heads propped up on ermine pillows, gazing out into the luminous blue sky which pressed against their gargantuan-size window. Mercy Merry, Mozart, all their belongings here now, stored in a massive closet—how could it get better? And from way up here, he couldn't see Rich Man Three's spread either, and that set well with him. He didn't want to be reminded of work. After all, he didn't feel particularly happy in those teaching sessions, slogging away with his stack of worn logic books close by, and getting nowhere. A wall of contradictions, he told Mercy Merry.

Not up here, though. Up here, with an interminable bed of pure white clouds laid out before them like infinity itself, there was absolutely nowhere to get to.

 Jack Smith's satirical novel *Hog to Hog* won the 2007 George Garrett Fiction Prize and was published by Texas Review Press in 2008. He has published stories in a number of literary magazines, including *Southern Review, North American Review, Texas Review, X-Connect, In Posse Review,* and *Night Train*. His reviews have appeared widely in such publications as *Ploughshares, Georgia Review, American Book Review, Prairie Schooner, Mid-American Review, Pleiades,* the *Missouri Review,* and *Environment* magazine. He has published two dozen articles in *Novel & Short Story Writer's Market* and over a dozen in *The Writer* magazine. His creative writing book, *Write and Revise for Publication: A 6-Month Plan for Crafting an Exceptional Novel and Other Works of Fiction,* was published in 2013 by Writer's Digest Books. His coauthored nonfiction environmental book entitled *Killing Me Softly* was published by Monthly Review Press in 2002. Besides his writing, Smith co-edits *The Green Hills Literary Lantern,* an online literary magazine published by Truman State University.

www.ingramcontent.com/pod-product-compliance
Lightning Source LLC
Chambersburg PA
CBHW030312180626
46810CB00003B/1042